John Creasey – M

Born in Surrey, England in 1908 were nine children, John Creasey grew up to be a true master story teller and international sensation. His more than 600 crime, mystery and thriller titles have now sold 80 million copies in 25 languages. These include many popular series such as *Gideon of Scotland Yard*, *The Toff*, *Dr Palfrey* and *The Baron*.

Creasy wrote under many pseudonyms, explaining that booksellers had complained he totally dominated the 'C' section in stores. They included:

Gordon Ashe, M E Cooke, Norman Deane, Robert Caine Frazer, Patrick Gill, Michael Halliday, Charles Hogarth, Brian Hope, Colin Hughes, Kyle Hunt, Abel Mann, Peter Manton, J J Marric, Richard Martin, Rodney Mattheson, Anthony Morton and *Jeremy York*.

Never one to sit still, Creasey had a strong social conscience, and stood for Parliament several times, along with founding the One Party Alliance which promoted the idea of government by a coalition of the best minds from across the political spectrum.

He also founded the British Crime Writers' Association, which to this day celebrates outstanding crime writing. The Mystery Writers of America bestowed upon him the Edgar Award for best novel and then in 1969 the ultimate Grand Master Award. John Creasey's stories are as compelling today as ever.

The Toff Series

- A Bundle for the Toff
- A Doll for the Toff
- A Knife for the Toff
- A Mask for the Toff
- A Rocket for the Toff
- A Score for the Toff
- Accuse the Toff
- Break the Toff
- Call the Toff
- Double for the Toff
- Feathers for the Toff
- Follow the Toff
- Fool the Toff
- Hammer the Toff
- Here Comes the Toff
- Hunt the Toff
- Introducing the Toff
- Kill the Toff
- Leave It to the Toff
- Kiss the Toff
- Model for the Toff
- Poison for the Toff
- Salute the Toff
- Stars for the Toff
- Terror for the Toff
- The Kidnapped Child
- The Toff among the Millions
- The Toff and Old Harry
- The Toff and the Crooked Copper
- The Toff and the Deadly Parson
- The Toff and the Deep Blue Sea
- The Toff and the Fallen Angels
- The Toff and the Golden Boy
- The Toff and the Great Illusion
- The Toff and the Lady
- The Toff and the Runaway Bride
- The Toff and the Sleepy Cowboy
- The Toff and the Spider
- The Toff and the Stolen Tresses
- The Toff and the Toughs
- The Toff and the Terrified Taxman
- The Toff and the Trip-Trip-Triplets
- The Toff at Butlins
- The Toff at the Fair
- The Toff Breaks In
- The Toff Goes On
- The Toff Goes to Market
- The Toff in New York
- The Toff in Town
- The Toff in Wax
- The Toff Is Back
- The Toff on Board
- The Toff on Fire
- The Toff Proceeds
- The Toff Steps Out
- The Toff Takes Shares
- Vote for the Toff

Murder Out of the Past (short stories)
The Toff on the Trail (short stories)

The Toff and the Spider

John Creasey

Copyright © 1965 John Creasey Literary Management Ltd.
© 2015 House of Stratus

All rights reserved. No part of this publication may be reproduced, stored in a retrieval system, or transmitted, in any form, or by any means (electronic, mechanical, photocopying, recording, or otherwise), without the prior permission of the publisher. Any person who does any unauthorised act in relation to this publication may be liable to criminal prosecution and civil claims for damages.

The right of John Creasey to be identified as the author of this work has been asserted.

This edition published in 2015 by House of Stratus, an imprint of
Stratus Books Ltd., Lisandra House, Fore Street,
Looe, Cornwall, PL13 1AD, U.K.
www.houseofstratus.com

Typeset by House of Stratus.

A catalogue record for this book is available from the British Library
and the Library of Congress.

ISBN 07551-3655-1
EAN 978-07551-3655-1

This book is sold subject to the condition that it shall not be lent, resold, hired out, or otherwise circulated without the publisher's express prior consent in any form of binding, or cover, other than the original as herein published and without a similar condition being imposed on any subsequent purchaser, or bona fide possessor.

This is a fictional work and all characters are drawn from the author's imagination.
Any resemblance or similarities to persons either living or dead are
entirely coincidental.

Chapter One

Lady Lost

The girl walked through the streets of the West End, but did not appear to look where she was going. She was bareheaded in the evening sunlight, and her hair was the colour of ripe corn. She wore a pleated white skirt and a simple creamy-white jumper. The neck of the jumper almost touched her cheek on one side and fell off the shoulder on the other. She walked beautifully. She had a good figure, not remarkable but nice; and she had slim legs and ankles. She wore heel-less moccasins and so made little sound as she passed along.

Many people noticed her when she first went by. Men with their wives glanced sideways, half-furtively, a few women glanced as if puzzled, young men in twos and threes nudged each other and half-prepared to become young wolves; perhaps the brightness of her cornflower-blue eyes made them feel slightly shamefaced. Middle-aged and elderly men, each one alone, watched her more openly, almost wistfully. Two deliberately got in her way, and one of these spoke. "Hi, Sis!" She did not seem to hear him. The other opened his mouth, but closed it and stepped quickly aside.

She walked past the queue waiting to go into a horror film at the big cinema at Piccadilly Circus, along Coventry Street and past the masses of people coming out of the big popular restaurants, across to Leicester Square. She turned along Charing Cross Road and then a side street which led to Shaftesbury Avenue, and went with purposeful purposelessness about the narrow streets of Soho. There most of the shops were shut, the better restaurants were guarded by closed doors and curtained windows, the little cafés looked messy and steamy with *espresso*, roadways and pavements were littered and hot after a humid day. Here, where narrow pavements were crowded, people brushed against the girl, some deliberately. A well-dressed man in his thirties stepped straight in front of her, and smiled.

"Did you come to see me?"

She stopped because he was in her way, but stared at him blankly. He was quite good-looking, and had a pleasant if rather ingratiating smile.

"I'll gladly go wherever you want to go," he offered.

She didn't speak, but moved to one side, so as to pass. Several people, men and women, stopped to stare. The man shrugged, and stood aside. The girl walked on, with everyone who had seen the little incident staring after her. The man disappeared into a doorway next to a window where a notice read:

Lessons in All Kinds of French.

An American woman, middle-aged, well-dressed in black and grey shantung and looking very cool, said to her husband: "Did you see that girl's face, George?"

"Sure," said George.

"Didn't you think she looked worried?"

"Sure," said George.

"Do you think she's all right?"

"Sure," repeated George. Then his eyes lit up, and he pointed across the road. "There's the place we want – Webbers." It was a small shop with faded green paint and faded gilt lettering on the dark green window. "Honey, they tell me that's the best restaurant in London for sea food"

He cupped his wife's elbow and led her across the road. By the time they reached the entrance to the restaurant, the girl had turned another corner.

She walked on.

She got back to Regent Street by devious streets, paused at the traffic flow, then crossed the road and went through one of the narrow streets to Piccadilly. Except to stop at kerbs or whenever she was impeded, she did not alter her pace, and all the time she stared fixedly ahead. As she drew near Piccadilly Circus a youthful-looking police constable saw her, and frowned. A dozen other men, idling, watched as she began to walk in exactly the same route that she had taken before.

A policewoman drew level with the policeman.

"Did you see her?" the constable asked.

"There are hundreds of hers," declared the policewoman.

"That girl in white, I mean."

"Davy boy, you're a big policeman now."

The youthful-looking constable grinned.

"A man's a man for all that! I mean the girl in white who's half-way across the road."

"I saw her in Frith Street," said the policewoman.

"I saw her here twenty minutes ago, and I think I saw her once before that."

"You're slipping if you can't be sure," said the policewoman. "You haven't seen a girl with a green jumper that sticks out a mile and a bottom that does a twist all of its own, have you? She skipped from a remand school this afternoon, and I'm told she's got an older sister who gives French lessons somewhere around here."

"I'll keep a special look-out," promised the young constable.

"I bet you will!"

Twenty minutes later, from the other side of Piccadilly, Police Constable David Ellis saw the girl in white yet again. She was about to cross the road. The policewoman, a rather plump, handsome girl, came and joined him.

"Yes, I saw her," she said. "I think there's something the matter with her, Davy."

"In what way?"

"She doesn't seem to be seeing anything or anybody. She looks as if she's in a kind of trance."

"Sleep-walking?"

"You know what I mean. Why don't you ask a C.I.D. man to keep an eye on her?"

"Not a bad idea," agreed P.C. Ellis.

A few minutes later two plain-clothes men from the Criminal Investigation Department came to pick up a message, for the West End was well populated with members of the Force, especially in the evening. The plain-clothes man who saw the girl in white, soon afterwards, was elderly and worldly-wise, the type who often claimed that he had seen everything. When he caught sight of the girl for the first time, however, he frowned, feeling sure that she was the one about whom the P.C. had talked. She *did* look as if she was sleep-walking, and that was absurd. She turned into a narrow street which cut right across Soho, and as he followed, a girl with an enormous bosom tightly encased in a blazing green sweater came out of a café. At the corner stood a policeman.

"That girl in green is wanted," the plain-clothes man said. "Hold her, Charlie."

He went on after the girl in white, reflecting that it would be almost impossible to think of two more different types of young woman – the one in white so slim, almost virginal, or pure; the one in green so fat, voluptuous, merry-eyed and grimy.

As the girl in white passed along the next street on her third peregrination a man stepped out of a doorway and took her arm.

"You'd better come with me, girlie," he said. "You're not safe out here on your own."

The girl turned and stared at him, tried to pull herself free, but could not. She showed no sign of alarm, only of resistance. The man pulled harder and she moved. He was smiling at her broadly. He was short, greasy-haired and olive-skinned and he had beautiful white teeth.

"Want six months for assault?" asked the plain-clothes man.

The other released the girl as if she were red-hot "I only wanted to help her!"

"You go and help yourself," ordered the plain-clothes man curtly.

The girl simply turned and went on. Her rescuer hurried and caught up with her, walking by her side without touching her. She knew he was there because she glanced at him several times, but she didn't speak and showed no sign of alarm. She took exactly the same route as she had before. Near Shaftesbury Avenue the detective tried again.

"Do you know where you're going?"

She didn't answer.

"Are you looking for someone?"

She didn't answer.

"I'm a police officer, and I'll be glad to help you." The words seemed to mean nothing to her. "You can't keep walking round and round like this," the man said, nettled. "Can I help you?" She ignored him.

He walked alongside her until they reached Regent Street again. A Black Maria was parked on one side, near the Café Royal, and the buxom green-clad brunette was climbing in; from the rear she looked enormous. A policeman standing by the back of the car almost gave her a hearty slap, but just stopped himself. The policewoman who had first talked about the girl in green wagged her finger at him.

The girl in white crossed the road, and the detective sergeant said to the policewoman: "I should try to have a talk with her. She won't take any notice of me. It's damned queer."

"Don't tell me you've never seen anything like it," remarked the policewoman sarcastically. "You're the man who's seen everything."

He grinned.

The policewoman caught up with the girl in white near Piccadilly Circus, where a lot of traffic was holding up a crowd by the kerb. Several more policemen were about here, and a man, half drunk, was singing in a crooning voice.

The policewoman took the girl's arm.

"Where are you going?" she asked briskly.

The girl tried to free herself, but did not use much strength. She said nothing.

"You can't wander about London like this, you know," the policewoman protested. She had been quick to see that the girl did not carry a handbag. "Where are you going to spend the night?"

The girl didn't speak.

"Have you any money with you?"

There was still no answer.

"If you haven't any money you'd better come with me," said the policewoman, firmly. She did not let the girl go, but signalled to the Black Maria which had made a complete circuit of the Circus and was now drawing up into the kerb. The plain-clothes man and two more policemen were close at hand. The doors of the big van opened, the policewoman hustled the girl forward. Almost before she or anyone else realised what had happened, the girl was inside the van and the policewoman was sitting beside her.

"Hallo, ducks," said the mischievous delinquent in green. "They're on the ball tonight, aren't they?"

"There's nothing to worry about," the policewoman said reassuringly. "We only want to help you. If you'll tell me your name and where you come from that will make it easier for us all."

The girl did not answer.

"What's up with her?" asked the irrepressible girl in green. "Not quite right on top?"

Chapter Two

A Request of the Toff

Less than half a mile away from Piccadilly Circus, at the time when the girl in white was taken in charge, the Honourable Richard Rollison sat at ease in the large room which served him as living-room, study and trophy room; and there was a small raised dining-alcove, too. Rollison lay back in an easy chair, a gentle breeze from an open window caressing his neck. His face was deeply tanned and a slight redness in his eyes suggested that he had seen too much of the sun that day. He had indeed. He had been playing cricket on a famous ground, and was now glad to relax and be a little pensive, for he had come to the simple if sad conclusion that he was not so young as he used to be; the day should soon come when he would make room for younger men to play the game beloved by flannelled fools. This reflection did not worry him too greatly. He had eaten; an iced lager glowed amber in the glass at his side as he looked idly through the pages of the *Evening News*. One headline on the front page ran:

MAN FOUND SHOT

The story read:

The body of an unknown man was found on Hampstead Heath this morning by two schoolboys who were bird-nesting. The man appeared to have been shot through the chest at close quarters. Superintendent Grice of Scotland Yard went to the scene of the discovery with officers from the Division, and Mr. Horace Wall, the Home Office Pathologist, was also on the scene.

Rollison glanced at the *stop press* news, and read:

Shot Man on Hamp. Heath. Police believe it is a case of murder. Gun used was .22

Rollison glanced up at the wall behind the big desk where he did most of his work. On the wall were countless souvenirs, more accurately called trophies of the hunt, the kind of hunt in which he had specialised for years: murder. There were lethal weapons of all kinds: guns, knives, blunt instruments and poisons; there were also other articles which in themselves were not sinister, such as silk stockings, pyjama sashes, chicken feathers and a host of others, all of which had been used with greater or less ingenuity to commit murder. There was a tiny gun, a .22, grey, squat. Either a man or a woman could use it, and a single bullet from it would bring instant death. He did not get up to examine this, but found himself wondering where the gun used in today's killing was at this moment.

Had the murderer got it, or had it been thrown away?

He was tempted to telephone the Yard and find out, but resisted. It was a fact that he could seldom restrain himself from asking questions about murder; the crime seemed to hypnotise him. But he was too lethargic tonight, and Grice, a good friend of his, would have had enough, too. If Rollison had not exerted himself so much earlier he might have got out his car and driven to the Heath to have a look round, but he decided against that also.

He finished the lager. Almost at once he heard the key at the front door. This was Jolly, his man, who had been out for the day. The door closed, Jolly appeared in the doorway, carrying his black bowler hat tightly against his waistcoat He wore a black coat and a pair of striped trousers, and a cravat; and he looked as if he had just come out of a band-box.

"Good evening, sir."

"Hallo, Jolly. Had a good day?"

"An interesting one in some ways, sir."

"That's good. What was interesting?"

"How did you get on, sir?" inquired Jolly, quickly enough to make it seem as if he had started his question at the same time as Rollison had started his.

"Fair," replied Rollison.

"I understand that you hit two sixes in your seventy-eight," murmured Jolly.

Rollison grinned.

"Your spies forgot to tell you that I was missed three times and ought to have been run out once. How's your aunt?"

Jolly, who was in the middle sixties, as he appeared to have been for the past twenty years, had an aunt in her eighties. He visited her very occasionally, always when the weather was good. She lived in St. John's Wood, still a pensioner of an old family which she had served most of her life.

"Very well indeed, sir. She expressed the wish today for a drive across Hampstead Heath and a picnic tea. It was most enjoyable." Jolly used a very small Austin, which was in fact Rollison's second car.

"Hampstead," echoed Rollison, nostalgically.

"*Very* interesting, sir," said Jolly.

After a pause, Rollison asked: "Have they found the gun yet?"

"No, sir."

"Found anything?"

"So far as I understand they are completely mystified. A night-long search has been arranged for the weapon, in view of the fact that there will be a full moon Mr. Grice has left the task to the Divisional officers, of course, but I understand that he will keep in touch. I quite enjoyed watching from a distance, sir, and my aunt was most excited."

"That's terrible," said Rollison. "Octogenarians shouldn't get excited. Do the police know who the man is yet?"

"No, sir."

"Did you see the body?"

"Yes, sir, but only as it was being placed into the ambulance, and I saw no more than the top of the man's head. He was grey-haired. The weather lured a great many people to the spot, naturally, and the work of the police has been considerably hampered. I understand that a photograph of the dead man has been sent to the newspapers and that it may appear on television in the news tonight."

"Switch on," ordered Rollison.

The face of the dead man was shown, soon afterwards. It was an interesting one, and Rollison had an impression of a scholarly and a gentle man. Even in the slackness of death the features had a kind of melancholy sadness. His hair was slightly curly, and on the fluffy side. A profile photograph showed that he had a high-bridged nose and a good chin.

"Just a little of the Roman about him," observed Rollison. "I should think the police are bound to learn who he is from that."

At half past eight next morning Rollison looked through the five newspapers which he took regularly. Only *The Times* failed to reproduce a photograph of the murdered man. At half past nine Rollison telephoned New Scotland Yard, and asked for Grice.

"He's over at Hampstead, sir," an inspector reported. "Can he call you when he gets back?"

"It's not important," said Rollison. "Haven't you caught that Hampstead murderer yet?"

"Not yet, sir," said the inspector, mildly.

"Any idea who the victim was?"

"Not yet, sir."

"Well I'll be damned," said Rollison. "No one's come forward, then."

"Obviously not," retorted the inspector, with a mild touch of malice.

"I asked for that," agreed Rollison humbly. "Don't hold it against me." He rang off, went to his bedroom, found that Jolly had laid out grey flannels and an M.C.C. blazer. He left the flat at ten o'clock, reached Lord's at a quarter to eleven, and spent a hot and unrewarding day in the field.

When he returned home at half past seven Jolly came out of the kitchen, a white apron over his clothes.

"Good evening, sir, I'm glad you're back promptly. Mr Grice would like a word with you, and said he would call again at seven forty-five. You have just time for your shower before then."

Rollison showered ...

At a quarter to eight precisely the telephone bell rang He took it for granted that Grice wanted something to do with the investigation at Hampstead, and was almost childishly pleased. After all, if the police actually asked for help, or at least co-operation, he could indulge his favourite pastime without anxiety. He sat on the corner of the desk, one leg swinging, and said: "Nice to know you can't do without me all the time, Bill. Do you know who it is yet?"

Grice asked, as if puzzled: "Who what is?"

"The victim."

"What victim?"

"Now don't be evasive," reproved Rollison. "The body found on Hampstead Heath."

Grice gave a snort of a laugh.

"Oh, that. No, we don't know yet, it's a bit of a teaser. But I didn't ring you to talk about murder, Rolly. Sorry to disappoint you."

Rollison was in fact disappointed, but knew that he would recover the quicker if he showed no sign of it to Grice.

"That's a great relief," he said. "I don't feel in the mood for murder. How can I help you?"

"As a matter of fact we've a queer little problem on our hands, and someone suggested that your Aunt Gloria might be able to help," Grice said. "She still runs the Marigold Club, doesn't she?"

Cautiously, Rollison replied: "Yes. But she isn't as active in it as she used to be. What's the job?"

"We've got a girl here who's in some kind of trouble and we don't know what it is," Grice went on. "She's a nice type, as far as we can judge – her clothes are of good quality, all made in France except her lingerie, and she gives the impression of quality, if you know what I mean." In fact Rollison was very puzzled, but he did not say so. "She was found wandering round the West End last night in a kind of daze – a trance, if you like. Our people brought her in. She wouldn't answer questions then, and she hasn't spoken since, except to murmur please and thank you. The doctors say that she's suffering from shock, but they don't know how long it will last. She's perfectly all right physically. Wall's seen her – you know Horace Wall – and he thinks she might come back to normal more quickly if she were in a less formal atmosphere."

"Where is she now?"

"At Charing Cross Hospital, under observation. If there is room at the Marigold Club, and she was able to mix with people of her own kind, it might help. Don't misunderstand me," went on Grice. "She's committed no offence. We were able to bring her in because she hadn't any money with her, so was without visible means of support. We simply want to help her. Everyone's a bit baffled."

"It sounds just the right job for my aunt," said Rollison. "I'll talk to her. Like the girl to be moved tonight?"

"I don't know that it's important, but on the whole I think it would be better. I know she will be very grateful, Rolly."

"The important thing is that you are," said Rollison in a weak and revealing moment. "Then you can tell me all about the mystery man of Hampstead Heath."

Grice laughed.

"When I've the time," he promised. "Will you call the hospital? Ask for the Night Sister, she knows all about the case."

"I will," promised Rollison.

Jolly appeared as he rang off, saw that he was about to dial another number, waited for the dialling and said: "Five minutes, sir?"

Rollison nodded.

A woman answered his call briskly.

"This is the Marigold Club."

"Is my aunt there, Maggie?" asked Rollison.

The Club's manageress said yes, asked him how he was, asked him to hold on and soon returned to say that Lady Gloria was coming. Rollison could picture his tall, white-haired, aristocratic-looking aunt, Lady Gloria Hurst, making her stately way to the telephone, mother-of-pearl lorgnette dangling on her shapely bosom, long grey skirt absurdly old-fashioned, a silver-topped ebony walking-stick supporting her. A year ago the Club had changed premises because of demolition and rebuilding; it was now housed in a fine old Georgian building in Belsize Square.

In a moment Lady Gloria said: "Good evening, Richard. It's been so long since I heard from you I quite thought that you had assumed that I had long been in my grave."

"You'll see me out of this world," declared Rollison. "Glory, I know of a young woman in trouble."

"If you mean a young woman who is going to have a baby, say so."

"Glory, Glory!" protested Rollison. "Such a thought hasn't entered my head. The police ..." he reported what Grice had told him, knowing exactly what her reaction would be. She had founded the Marigold Club many years ago as a kind of club-cum-home-from-home for single women or married women who for one reason or another needed to live alone for a while. "... and if she is going to have a baby, don't blame me."

"I should hope that there would be no need to," said Lady Gloria. "What time will you bring her?"

"Let's say in an hour and a half," Rollison said. He went to the hospital immediately after dinner, driving the Austin. After all a Rolls-Bentley would be too ostentatious, and might even create some nervous reaction in the girl. The Night Sister at the hospital was expecting him; she was a tall, angular, somewhat forbidding woman with a beautifully modulated voice. She led him to a small room, a pleasant lounge, where the girl was waiting. A diminutive nurse sat in a corner working on some reports, and the girl sat in a small armchair, staring at the plain green wall opposite.

Rollison was startled by the way she sat, so absolutely still. Her hands were folded on her lap. She did not look round when the door opened, and did not speak when she was spoken to. The most remarkable thing was that she glowed with health. She was not really beautiful but had a lovely complexion. Her clear cornflower-blue eyes and striking corn-coloured hair were most disconcerting. The Sister handed him a sealed envelope. The official diagnosis is in there," she said. "She will be going to a place where she will be assured of absolute rest, won't she?"

"*Most* certainly," Rollison assured her.

"I'm very glad," the Sister said. She led the way to the door.

"Please follow us," she called to the girl.

The girl sat staring.

"Bring her downstairs, Nurse," ordered the Sister, and went out of the room. "I've never known anyone quite like her, Mr. Rollison. She isn't deaf. She can talk, although she only uses monosyllables. She *has* eaten, but not very much. All the usual tests are normal – temperature, blood-pressure, pulse, heart. So far we haven't been able to get a word of explanation out of her. Dr. Wall and Dr. Simister, our resident psychologist, say that she has suffered some kind of acute shock."

"And is all of that in this report?" Rollison held up the envelope.

"Everything."

"Thank you."

They went outside into the street and Rollison waited by the side of the little car. The nurse came out with the girl by her side doing exactly what she was told; the nurse's guiding hand seemed very gentle. Several people, passing by, stared with a curiosity which would not have seemed out of place the previous night. The nurse led her towards the open door of the car.

"Please get inside," she said.

The girl in white hesitated, then lowered her head and got in; she was very clumsy while doing so, first bumping her head, then banging her shins, but she did not complain. Soon she sat next to Rollison, who started the engine and drove the few yards towards the Strand, then swung into Trafalgar Square. The girl sat staring straight ahead.

"Wonderful evening," Rollison remarked lightly. "And I should think the pigeon population of Trafalgar Square has doubled, wouldn't you?"

She didn't answer.

Rollison drove through the Admiralty Arch and down the shady, lovely Mall.

"I think this is one of the nicest parts of London," he observed. "Have you ever watched the ducks in St. James's Park?"

She said nothing.

"Buckingham Palace isn't the most handsome building in London, but I see that the Royal Family is in residence. The Royal Standard's flying."

She *spoke:* "*Is* it?" she asked.

She did not utter another word but Rollison congratulated himself and tried to pretend that from that moment on she took more interest in where she was going. He even thought that she listened whenever he told her where they were and what landmark they passed. It was a remarkable experience, none the less. Soon they were on the other side of Piccadilly, in the streets of Mayfair which had a charm and grace of their own. He drove along Gresham Terrace, where he had his own flat, and soon turned into Belsize Square. He noticed a man on a motor-scooter but thought nothing of it. There was a parking space outside the Marigold Club, as usual in the evening, and he pulled into it and said brightly: "Here we are! And I know you're going to like Lady Gloria very much indeed."

He got out, went to her door, opened it and handed her out; again she moved clumsily, and he just saved her from bumping her head.

"Ooops!" he said, inanely, and turned round.

He noticed that the motor-scooterist had turned into the Square and was slowing down. He also noticed that the rider, a man in his twenties, was sitting astride the machine and staring along the pavement. He saw the man's right hand slide into his pocket, very slowly. Nine out of ten, perhaps ninety-nine out of a hundred people would not have noticed that, and even if they had would have assumed that the scooter rider was reaching for his cigarettes. But there was an intensity about his manner, a stealth of movement which rang a warning bell in Rollison's mind.

He thrust the girl back, nearer the car. She banged her head and cried out in pain.

A gun appeared in the scooterist's hand, and he was levelling it.

Chapter Three

.22

The girl was falling, Rollison was ducking, the man on the motor-scooter was pointing the gun. In that instant it was like a tableau held for a split second before all the actors in it moved. Rollison shouted at the girl: *"Don't get up!"* He crouched behind the open door of the car, able to see the man with the gun, but in no immediate danger. The only people in the Square were on the other side. *"Don't get up!"* he bellowed again, and then crept forward to get a better view of what was going on in the Square.

A window banged and a woman shouted: "Get along with you! Get along!" It was like someone shouting at a cat or dog, but this was a grey-haired woman leaning out of the window and shaking her fists at the motor-scooterist. This was Lady Gloria in battle mood.

"Glory! Get inside!" called Rollison urgently. Then he heard the scooter's engine start up. The rider swung the machine away from the kerb, and for a few seconds was out of sight, but he was coming this way. Rollison snatched his hand from his pocket, gold cigarette case held tight, and hurled the case over the top of the Austin towards the motor-scooterist. He missed by inches. The machine roared past. The case glistened and clattered. The rider fired twice, and the shots barked. Glass smashed. Lady Gloria was still shouting angrily, the two people on the other side of the road were standing and gaping. The door of the Marigold Club opened and a middle-aged woman came running.

Rollison said gruffly. "I'd like to break his neck." As he backed away he saw the girl crouching on the floor. "It's all right now, the danger's over," he assured her.

She did not answer, but stared up at him with such piteous entreaty that it was almost frightening. Her lips were twitching. Terror spoiled that unspoiled face. Her whole body was aquiver with a fear greater than any girl should know. He could hear her teeth chattering.

"Now, take it easy," he made himself say. "There's nothing to worry about. He's gone."

The chattering of her teeth sounded much louder. Rollison was glad when the middle-aged woman reached them.

She was Margaret Lister, who now managed the Marigold Club and probably knew more about the problems and the anxieties of lonely women and girls than anyone outside the Probation Service.

"I'll look after her," she said.

"Thanks, Maggie."

"You'd better go and see Lady Gloria."

"After you've gone in," said Rollison.

The girl's mouth was still twitching, but she had closed her eyes. Rollison helped her up. Margaret Lister put an arm round her and started off towards the open door, which looked as if it led into an ordinary house, not into a club. Rollison peered up and down the street, his ears were tuned to catch the first clatter of the scooter's engine, but he heard nothing. The couple, man and woman, came hurrying across the Square.

"What on earth happened?"

"Was there *shooting?*" an elderly woman looked scared.

"I shouldn't worry about it," Rollison said.

"Not worry! The police must be sent for at once."

"You couldn't be more right," said Rollison. "Would you care to find a telephone, call Scotland Yard, and ask for Superintendent Grice? GRICE. If he's not in, his assistant will be. I've an urgent job to do."

Rollison beamed at them and went to the other side of the little car. The quicker he had an official report made the better, but he wanted to see the extent of the damage and check if there were any clues which he could see before the police.

The driving window of the car was smashed and scarred, and a bullet hole was at head level. He looked down on the leather seat, which had a few tiny fragments of glass on it, and the bullet. He did not touch the bullet, for it told him all he wanted to know while it lay there.

It was a .22, same calibre as that which had killed the man on Hampstead Heath. He thought: *"It can't be."*

He did not convince himself, however, for it seemed far, far too much for coincidence. He heard the man and woman talking, and the woman said: *"Here's a policeman!"*

A constable was hurrying along the Square. Now other people were standing about, more of them had been at the front of the houses than he had realised. He looked above the heads of several of them and winked at the policeman, then pointed to the Marigold Club. As question after question was flung at him and at the other two sightseers, he went into the Club but did not close the door.

It was not long before the policeman was in the hall with him.

"Tell your chaps that we're looking for a man in his twenties, dark-haired, slender, wearing an Italian style suit pale brown in colour. The bridge of his nose is broken or else the natural shape is a bit peculiar."

"So you got a good look at him, sir."

"As he passed at about forty miles an hour," said Rollison, and omitted to add that he himself had been ducking behind the Austin. "Ask Division to tell Mr. Grice quickly, will you? Say that a .22 bullet nearly killed me."

"I see, sir," said the policeman. He now looked dazed, but he recovered as he began to dial at the telephone in the hall.

"It can't be," Rollison said *sotto voce* as he turned away.

"What did you say, sir?"

"I'm going upstairs to see how the patient is," said Rollison. "I don't think she was hurt this time, but I'd better make sure."

He hurried up the stairs. At the head of them, Lady Gloria appeared from a doorway leading from a large room. She stood upright as a post, black stick just touching the ground, rather like a retired field marshal who thought it time he rehearsed taking the salute. She was a fine old woman with a matriarchal face and a matriarchal manner. Most people who met her these days deemed her an autocrat, and no doubt she was; but she had no terrors for a man who had once been dandled on her lap.

"How is she?" inquired Rollison.

"From the glimpse I had of her, in a very bad state of nerves," said Lady Gloria. "I am about to telephone for Dr. Halliday, unless you have some better idea."

"I don't feel as if I've got an idea in my head," said Rollison.

"From what I heard you saying downstairs your memory is still reasonably good," declared his aunt. After a pause, she added: "How are you, Richard?"

"I couldn't be better," Rollison said. He gripped her hand and kissed her cheek. "Don't be an old goose, nothing will happen to me."

"I wish I could feel as sure as you do," said Lady Gloria. Then her voice hardened. "Don't stand there doing nothing. I wish to telephone Dr. Halliday."

Rollison stepped aside. The policeman was talking to someone down in the hall. Rollison went into the room where Margaret Lister was sitting on the edge of a single bed and looking rather anxiously at the girl on it. She had loosened the girl's skirt at the waist, and was holding her right hand. The victim of the attack was trembling violently, as if she couldn't stop. She stared straight at the ceiling, not at the woman or at Rollison.

"That's pretty bad," murmured Rollison. "Any ideas, Maggie?"

"I think we'd better get the doctor to give her a sedative as soon as possible."

"Yes," Rollison said. "We won't learn anything from her today, anyhow. She wasn't hurt, was she?"

"There's a scratch on the back of her neck, that's all."

Rollison nodded, took another look at the girl, whose face was aquiver, whose lips were trembling, whose eyes were blank except for remembered fear. He was profoundly grateful that he had not been directly responsible for her leaving the hospital. She ought really to go back, but he still doubted whether Maggie or Lady Gloria would want her to leave. They would much prefer to accept some measure of responsibility, and would want to help. He went downstairs as a car pulled up outside, and at the same time a youthful-looking man with a mop of untidy brown hair appeared in the front doorway. Words bubbled out of him.

"It *is* Mr. Rollison, isn't it? I'm from the *Daily Globe,* Mr. Rollison. Is it true that you were fired at?"

"Twice," said Rollison firmly. "And you'll be shot if you don't make way for the police." He saw three heavily built men bearing down on the house, they came from a patrol car which must have been summoned by radio. "If you hang around you should be able to pick up quite a lot of odds and ends, though."

"Then that's what I'll do. Any statement from you, sir?" Eager eyes in a bright young face told of enthusiasm.

Rollison frowned. "Yes," he said at last. "All crime is antisocial."

Everyone laughed, including the policemen, two in uniform and one in plain-clothes. He told them as fully as he could what had happened, but omitted to say that he thought the bullet had been a .22. They would soon find that out.

When more police arrived, the section of pavement and road near the Austin was cordoned off, photographers took their pictures and a large crowd was gathering. The young reporter wandered among them, starry-eyed. A bustling elderly man carrying a black bag arrived, and a policeman tried to stop him.

"Doctor," growled the elderly man, and pushed past. He saw Rollison. He was a bushy-haired, bushy-eyebrowed, burly man who had known Lady Gloria most of his life and Rollison from the day he had been born. "Might have known you were involved," he said accusingly.

"Hallo, Doc," said Rollison brightly.

He went into the Square, ignoring the dozens of reporters who now asked him questions, saw a black car turn a corner, and recognised the driver who was alone: it was Superintendent William Grice of New Scotland Yard. Rollison startled everyone nearby by breaking into a run, and Grice jammed on the brakes as Rollison dodged in front of the car. Rollison opened the door next to the Yard man and beamed: "Can we have a chat for ten minutes, Bill?"

Grice accelerated as the door slammed, and no one appeared to recognise him. He turned a corner and headed for Piccadilly, near Green Park. There was ample room to park in a side street and he pulled up. Rollison was staring at him intently, and Grice said almost irritably: "What's the matter with my face?"

"As faces go it's all right," conceded Rollison. "But as a profile it's almost parental to the chap who shot at our unknown damsel. Is your nose natural or did someone break it?"

"As far as I know it's natural."

"Just like the motor-scooterist's," said Rollison.

In fact Grice's nose had a high bridge which was slightly twisted, and the skin there was very tight, so that it looked almost white. He had a sallow complexion but a good skin. His hair had once been brown and was now greying. The far side of his face was badly scarred, where a plastic bomb had blown up and nearly killed him; the fact that the bomb had been intended for Rollison had created a kind of bond between these two men. Grice was saying, heavily: "I got the message about the motor-cyclist as I was driving here. *And the description.*"

"It was a scooter, remember, not a cycle."

"Yes – my mistake." Grice was turning round in his seat and staring at Rollison. "What's this about a .22 bullet?"

Rollison put his hand in his pocket, opened it and let the little lead cylinder roll about on his palm. Grice stared as if it was something he hated.

"There's the little beauty, and it's the same size as the little beauty which killed your man at Hampstead. I keep telling myself that it couldn't be from the same gun but I'd like to be sure. How long will it be before we can check? Need you worry yet about the routine at the Club?"

"No," said Grice. "Let's get to the Yard."

In the Ballistics Department there was a variation of a microscope which enabled the operator to compare bullets. Every bullet fired by every gun, no matter how short the barrel, carried its own identification, at least as positively as the identification of fingerprints on human beings. A short, dapper, bald-headed man was in charge that evening, and he put the bullets to the test. One taken from the body of the man found dead at Hampstead was cut in half; that which Rollison had brought from the Austin seat was cut in the same way. Then, on the machine, the halves from each different bullet were brought together.

Grice looked at them intently through the magnifying instrument. Rollison watched, trying to pretend that he didn't wish he were in Grice's position.

Grice drew back.

"Take a look," he invited.

Rollison took his place, peered at the two halves of the bullet, watched as the operator moved them away from each other and then closed them again. These two halves made one whole, for they had identical markings. There was no shadow of doubt about it.

Chapter Four

Girl in Danger

Grice, in his office which overlooked the Thames, sat back at his desk and looked evenly at Rollison. Outside the river traffic had almost stopped, but the floodlighting was on at the County Hall and the Festival Hall and the great new office blocks. Cars were few and far between but in the distance there was a continual drone of engines.

"The worst aspect is the danger for that girl," Grice said.

"Don't I know it."

"Do you want her to stay at the Marigold Club?"

"It's as safe as anywhere provided it's watched," reasoned Rollison. "You'd better attach one of your policewomen to the staff for the time being, hadn't you? There's a back entrance which wants watching, too, but that's no problem now."

"No," Grice said. He flicked one of the halves of the bullets. It rolled along his desk and fetched up at a file of reports. "No. This girl might possibly be a vital witness in a murder case. We'll watch her no matter how many men it needs. Will you tell Lady Gloria the whole truth?"

"Yes."

"If she prefers to let the girl go back—" began Grice.

"She won't," interrupted Rollison. "I shouldn't try to take her away now, Bill. She'll be better off at the Marigold Club, and I can go in and out of there much better than a nursing home or a hospital. What we want—" he broke off.

"What you want is a bait to draw the attackers again," said Grice drily. "I know, and that's what I'm afraid of. It's what Lady Gloria ought to fear, too. But on the whole I think it would be better to let the girl stay where she is." He picked up a folder in which were two sheets of paper, both buff forms. "Here are the reports on the girl. Negative."

"I've got copies," Rollison said.

"I wonder if she saw the shooting, and that caused the shock," suggested Grice.

"Could be," said Rollison, pensively. "And she was so terrified when she heard today's shooting that her shock might well be due to gunfire of one kind or another. I can give you a few other oddments for the file, too. She's probably used to getting in and out of a car with bigger doors than my Austin, either a large car or a car with bigger openings, which means a foreign one or even a small van. She bumps herself too much on that car I've been using. If she thought about what she's doing she would be all right but she moves and walks automatically, and so she keeps bumping her head and her shins."

Grice made notes.

"Thanks. Next?"

"She's left-handed."

Grice raised his eyebrows.

"Sure?"

"All her natural movements start with the left hand, not her right."

"Good point," said Grice, almost pompously. "Any idea about her nationality?"

"She could be American or Scandinavian, but I wouldn't like to gamble," Rollison said. "The one time she spoke to me her English was good, but she might have been educated here even if she isn't English. If I had to guess I would say she isn't. How much have you seen of her?"

"Not much."

Rollison said: "Enough to want to get the man who frightened her so badly, I hope."

"Rolly, you can afford to get emotionally involved in this kind of thing, but I can't," Grice answered gruffly. "I feel terribly sorry for her, but that's as far as I'll go."

"Thanks, Bill. Any word or clue at all about the body on the Heath?"

Grice said: "No, we haven't a thing. It's almost certain the body was moved to the spot where we found it, we're practically certain that the killing didn't take place there, but we can't be positive. The bullets were fired at close quarters, but – well, would you like to see the body?"

"Yes, please," Rollison said.

That rather sad face, caught perfectly by the photographer, had no skin blemish at all. In death the man looked younger than he had in the picture. His hair was fluffy and silky. The bullets had been fired at very close quarters, and the holes made were quite small; there had been little bleeding. He had been shot through a shirt and a vest, and the shirt showed faint scorch marks. Each bullet had entered the heart.

"We can't find any trace of Hampstead Heath soil on his shoes," Grice said. They were now in a little ante-room next to the morgue and he picked up a pair of well-made brown shoes. "See the soles? If he'd walked on the Heath we would have seen something." He picked up one or two little plastic bags. "Here are the scrapings taken from the shoes and in that other bag from the nails. Nothing at all. The shoes are of good English make, but they weren't made to measure. We're trying to trace them, but tens of thousands of that identical shape and size are sold each year. The clothes are English, too, also bought off the peg."

"As new as the shoes?" asked Rollison.

Grice took down a suit which hung from a hook inside a plastic container.

"Pretty new," he answered.

"Very new, surely," said Rollison. "So are the girl's clothes."

Grice said: "Are you sure?"

"Well if not new, very little used," amended Rollison. "Bill, it might be worth your while working on airports and coastal ports to find out if anyone recalls seeing the man and the girl together."

"I'll fix it." Grice lifted a telephone. *"Information,* please." After a moment's pause, he went on: "Will you send this message and request for information by teleprinter to all airports and seaports and main-line stations." He gave the message in precise words which were exactly what was needed, and rang off. That was like Grice: he never wasted a word or a minute. "Anything else, Rolly?"

"Bill."

"Yes."

"Why are you holding out on me?"

"But I'm not."

"You know who the dead man is."

"I do *not.*"

After a pause, Rollison relaxed.

"Sorry, Bill. I thought you might be pulling a fast one. Well, I ought to go and make peace with Lady Gloria."

"Give her my regards," said Grice.

Lady Gloria, far from wanting apologies and reassurances was very nearly excited. She had very clear grey eyes and for a woman in her eighties, a remarkably good complexion, although her skin was lined in a criss-cross which cut very deep. There were spots of colour on her cheeks and a glint in her eyes.

"Provided the police watch the Club very carefully, Richard, I will certainly look after the young woman. Maggie has arranged to move her to a small but very charming top-floor room, and we shall do everything we can to help her when she comes round. Dr. Halliday thinks that she should come out of—what was the ridiculous word he used?"

"Sedation?"

"That's right, sedation. She should come out of it in the morning, probably around noon. I have only one request to make."

"Yes?"

"Tell your friend Grice that it is one thing to send his regards, another to prove that he means it. I quite understand that he must station a policewoman here, and in fact it might be advisable to have two. I hope he will make sure that they will fit in with the Club, and not stick out like a sore thumb. We want this young woman to feel that she is among friends, not among servants!"

"So she's top drawer, Glory?"

"She appears to be well-bred. Everything about her suggests that."

"What about her clothes?"

"Of good quality and bought at an expensive place I should imagine, but not remarkable. In very good taste, nevertheless."

"Nationality?"

"Once we have persuaded her to talk we should know more about that for certain. I would think—"

"Don't hesitate," urged Rollison.

"I must say that your manners do not appear to improve with the passing years," rebuked Lady Gloria. "Judging from her complexion, her colouring and her hair, she could be Italian, Spanish or southern French."

"But she has corn-coloured hair?" Rollison scoffed.

"Maggie tells me that her hair is dyed," announced Lady Gloria. "In any case, don't tell me that the cornflower-blue eyes are unusual in southern Europe. They are indeed, but they are not by any means unique."

"No, Aunt," said Rollison humbly. "But aren't you guessing rather freely about her nationality?"

"No more than you often guess," retorted his aunt. "I think you will find that she uses a make-up base which is peculiar to hot countries. Maggie feels quite sure."

"And who am I to question Maggie! Let me know when the invalid begins to sit up and take notice, won't you?"

"Richard."

"Yes, Aunt?"

"I do not wish you to use this young woman as a bait to draw unwonted attentions to this place. Nor do I wish you to treat the Marigold Club as if it were an extension of your apartment."

"No, indeed," said Rollison fervently. "I will attempt no such thing, I promise you."

Both Grice and Lady Gloria had jumped to the conclusion that he would try to use the Marigold Club as a place to which to lure the man who had attempted to kill the girl. And no doubt he would, if he had the chance. The trouble was that he appeared to have no clue at all, but as he drove home in a taxi – for the police had taken over the Austin and were likely to keep it for a few days – he smoked and pondered and came to a conclusion which did not worry but excited him, as danger often did. There was no need to use the unknown girl or the Marigold Club as a bait. He had seen the man on the motor-scooter and could identify him. No one else, with the possible exception of Aunt Gloria, had seen him so clearly. He, Rollison, would probably be as good if not a better bait than the girl or the Club.

He paid off the cabby and went whistling up to his flat, more content than he had been for some hours.

Murder had been done and more murder had been intended. That second attack had only one purpose: to kill the girl. It might have been to stop her from talking, obviously, or there might be some other motive. If it had been simply to silence her, then now he, Rollison, had to be silenced. His problem was to let the man on the motor-scooter know that he had been seen. Rollison put the key into the lock of his door, still whistling. Yet by this time he was a little puzzled, for Jolly usually heard him coming, and usually had the door open and was waiting; that was a time-honoured custom in the evenings. Tonight the door was locked, and there was no sign or sound of Jolly.

The sixth sense – which was really the result of long experience, which had warned Rollison that the man on the scooter had been about to draw a gun – took over again. He pushed the door back and stepped swiftly to one side.

Nothing happened; no sound came.

"I could be making this up," he murmured aloud, but did not close the door behind him as he stepped forward. He wished he had some weapon. "Jolly," he called.

There was no answer.

"*Jolly!*"

There was still no answer.

Rollison reached the door which led to the big room and looked inside. A lamp was alight by his chair, but the main lights were off. The trophy wall had a sinister appearance in the shadowy gloom. He turned into the passage which led to the domestic quarters. A light was on in the kitchen, too.

"Jolly," he called. His tone was lighter now as if he were puzzled but not troubled or alarmed. He did not expect an answer. The kitchen was empty and the light unit came from the larder. Rollison picked up a rolling-pin, pushed it under his jacket, and went first into Jolly's bedroom, then the bathrooms, the spare room and finally his own bedroom. Each was empty. In each a single light burned just as it would if Jolly were home.

Rollison thought: "He must have slipped out for a few minutes."

There was no note. Jolly must have been expecting him at any time, and would not have gone out without leaving a message.

Rollison went into the big room. One newspaper was folded on a table by the side of his chair, and one, half-opened, was in the chair as if Jolly had been reading there and had got up in a hurry. Each paper carried the story of the Hampstead murder, none mentioned the attack on the girl. But there was a brief paragraph in the *Evening News*.

MYSTERY GIRL

A fair-haired girl apparently suffering from loss of memory was taken into custody by the police last night. No charge was made. The police are anxious to trace relatives or friends of the girl who is described as ...

The description was the official one.

Rollison dropped the newspaper down on to the chair again. He thought he heard a rustle of movement, but he had been in every room and was sure that no one was inside the flat. Imagination could play strange tricks, but it wasn't imagination that Jolly was missing.

He searched again, but saw no one and found no explanation of the rustling. Jolly puzzled him, but he tried to reassure himself. He checked that both doors were locked; when Jolly came back he would have to ring or knock to get in. That done, Rollison went to his chair to sit down, and picked up the paper which was spread over the seat.

He jumped back as the snake spat at him.

Chapter Five

Deadliness

It was an adder, an ordinary English adder with a bite venomous enough to kill. It had drawn back and was coiled up again. The lacework-like skin of the back seemed to shimmer; the tongue was out as it hissed and spat. Rollison's heart thumped wildly as he drew farther away. It couldn't harm him now, thank God, for he could tackle it but if he had sat down it might have been fatal.

It was beginning to weave about.

He backed into the passage leading to the domestic quarters; in reach was a broom cupboard where Jolly kept a broom and a vacuum cleaner, as well as Rollison's cricket bats. The adder began to move, and to slide down the side of the chair. Rollison turned a ball-marked bat upside down and went back. He didn't want to kill the thing on the carpet; if he could get it into the fireplace or even into the kitchen or bathroom it would be a cleaner job. At cricket-bat length he poked at it. It spat and weaved. He gave a flick and it rose into the air and fell half-way between him and the fireplace. Now it was seething with anger. He approached again. The thing could get a hold on the handle and climb up it. Rollison shuddered and tried again. The snake struck the brass Regency fender, hovered on the top and flopped on the side.

"Got you," Rollison said softly. He turned the bat round and used it like a club. As he killed the thing he kept shuddering. That was partly from nervous reaction. He drew back and looked at the bottom of the bat which was messy with the creature's blood. He went to a corner cupboard, opened it to get a drink – and a second snake dropped from a shelf.

"God!" he cried, and darted back. Glasses fell and smashed, the snake wriggled towards a corner as if it in turn was frightened. Rollison didn't waste time worrying about the carpet but smashed the creature where it was.

He felt very tense, and knew that all his colour had gone.

If there were two there might be three or more, and the others might be hidden anywhere. Three or four or more – this was deadly. He stood in the middle of the room wishing more than ever that Jolly was here, and then was overcome by a feeling of deep alarm – for Jolly. Where was his man?

He thought he heard more rustling and darted a glance over his shoulder, saw nothing, but reminded himself that he couldn't be sure what else he might find. He needed help, and the police were best for this emergency. He stretched out his hand for the telephone on the desk, scanning the trophy wall; that was a good hiding-place, two or three snakes might be entwined among the trophies. He touched the instrument and it rang. He snatched his hand away, feeling the quivering from the ringing. It rang on and on, *brrr-brrr, brrr-brrr*. He gulped, wiped his forehead with the back of his hand, took another look round and picked up the telephone. He stepped farther away from the desk so that nothing could catch him unawares.

"Rollison," he said.

There was no answer.

"This is Richard Rollison—"

He heard the sound of the caller ringing off, and the line went dead. He stood with the instrument in his hand for fully a quarter of a minute, then replaced it slowly. He was cold. When he wiped his forehead again, it was wet. He went across to the corner cabinet, treading on broken glass, antique cut glass of great sentimental value. He poured out a whisky, added only a splash of soda and tossed it down. Soon he moved back to the desk. He looked about the foot of it and about the chairs and other furniture, afraid of what might be concealed in dark corners. This time the bell did not ring. He dialled Whitehall 1212, and it seemed a long time before a man announced: "Scotland Yard."

"Mr. Grice, please."

"One moment."

He held on. Grice might have gone home, but his deputy would do.

Why didn't someone speak?

"Grice," Grice answered.

"Bill, this is Rollison."

After a pause, Grice said: "Are you all right?"

"Only just," Rollison said. "Will you—" He gulped, and then began to feel better; the whisky was taking effect or else his nerve was stiffening of its own accord. "Bill, I came back to my flat to find Jolly gone and two adders mixing it with the furniture and the hard liquor. What would you suggest we do about looking for more?"

After a pause, Grice said: "Adders?" in a curious voice, as if he didn't really believe that he was saying it.

"The venomous, not the mathematical kind," Rollison explained. "I would like some help in looking round, preferably from someone who knows what tricks the little jokers get up to."

"Good God!" exclaimed Grice. He might almost have said: *You're serious.* "You be careful. I'll send someone over quick as light."

Rollison put down the telephone and wiped his forehead again. He still felt better, but it would be a long time before he got over the shock. Moreover, the second deeper anxiety about Jolly was catching up with him.

He heard a car turn into the street, very fast. This would be a patrol car, already contacted by the Yard. He went to the front door, watching every step he took, knowing that he might have killed the only two snakes in the flat, but it would be a long time before he felt sure. He opened the door. Car doors slammed downstairs and soon he heard footsteps. It was not until he saw a policeman's helmet approaching up the stairs, bobbing in a comical way as the wearer came up two at a time, that he really felt that he could relax.

Two men, one of them pulling on a pair of leather gloves, reached the landing.

"All right, sir," one man said; obviously Grice had briefed him well. "We'll see to it. Will you tell us just what happened?"

Rollison told him, and saw the way the eyes of each man rounded at sight of the two battered snakes. Then two more men arrived, and during the next fifteen minutes Rollison saw the whole flat turned upside down, every drawer emptied and every piece of furniture moved, to make sure that no more snakes were hidden here. None was. The job was nearly finished when another man came into the flat.

It was Grice.

Grice said: "I've had a call put out for Jolly, but nothing's in yet."

"Thanks," said Rollison. His mouth was dry. "Not nice people, are they?"

"It shook you, didn't it?"

"Badly."

"I suppose it must be connected—" Grice broke off.

"It doesn't have to be."

"But it probably is," insisted Grice. "Who else would be likely to choose this moment to want to get rid of you? You saw that man on the motor-scooter, and—" He smoothed down his hair before going on: "Well, we can soon put that right. We can give the Press a statement that you've given us the description, and then there'll be no point in trying to kill you." He went on explosively: "How the hell is it *you* always get involved in this kind of ruthlessness? Why can't you settle for a straightforward murder?"

"I wish I knew," Rollison said. "Bill, forget it."

"Forget what?"

"That statement to the police."

"But it's the only way to make sure that you're not attacked again!"

"It wouldn't make anything sure, but it might make difficulties in negotiating for Jolly." Rollison gulped. "I'll be vulnerable for a long time. Let's make as much use of my vulnerability as we can." He heard two men coming from the kitchen, looked round and smiled. "Have you chaps finished?"

"You can be absolutely sure that there's no more here, sir. We even turned the dustbin inside out, on the fire-escape landing."

"Ah," said Rollison. "Thanks. I hope I never have to do the same for you." He watched with a set smile as the men went out, and then turned to Grice. "Your chaps have been very good, Bill. Thanks." He spoke jerkily, knowing that he wasn't at all himself. So he tried to force a grin to look natural. "I shall be all right, once we've found Jolly. I wonder how—"

The telephone bell rang, sharp and insistent as always, and making him jump; it was a relief that Grice jumped, too. Rollison moved across and picked up the receiver.

"Is Mr. Grice there, please?" a man asked.

"Hold on," said Rollison, and handed over. He moved away, looking down at the spot which the officers had washed so as to get rid of the squashy mess made by the snakes. It was something in the way Grice said: *"What's that?"* which made him turn his head, and he caught Grice looking at him in a startled, anxious way. He gave up all pretence at not watching Grice, heard him say: "Yes," several times, and finally: "Right away." He put down the receiver, and Rollison stood with his teeth and his fists clenched, with fear for Jolly in his mind, and a premonition that Grice had received bad news.

"They've found Jolly," Grice said.

"Ah."

"Badly hurt."

Rollison echoed: "Hurt?"

"Badly, but not fatally."

After a pause, Rollison asked roughly: "How the hell do you know whether it will be fatal. Where is he?"

"Westminster Hospital."

Rollison said: "You can explain on the way." He hurried to the front door without waiting to see whether Grice was following. Grice was, carrying his hat and swinging it. Outside stood a policeman in uniform and Grice nodded to him. Rollison hardly noticed him, and did not nod or smile. Downstairs another policeman was on duty in the hall. A car drew up as Rollison and Grice stepped into the street.

"Here's the fingerprint squad," Grice said. "They might pick something up at your flat."

"Which is your car?"

"The Rover," replied Grice, who often used a police car, not his own. They got in, with Rollison staring bleakly ahead. "Jolly was taken into Westminster Hospital twenty minutes ago, as an accident case. He had been left near a telephone booth and an emergency call was made from it by someone unknown."

Rollison didn't speak.

"Head and leg injuries mostly and I was assured that they were not likely to be fatal."

Rollison said: "Thanks, Bill. Get a move on, will you?"

"There is no reason to suppose that the injuries will prove fatal," a surgeon said. "They are serious, mind you and there is no way of guaranteeing that there will not be a change for the worse, but certainly no reason to anticipate one. The leg injuries may have been caused by a car which ran him down. The head injuries appear to have been caused as a result of an impact or a fall."

"Do you mean that they could have been inflicted with a blunt instrument?" asked Grice formally.

"Yes, superintendent," the surgeon replied.

Horace Wall, whose collar was undone and who wore old leather slippers, came to Rollison at the flat just after midnight. By that time the fingerprint squad had done its job, and the flat was looking almost normal again, except that it could never be normal without Jolly. Grice had been gone for half an hour, but the police were still on duty. Rollison had realised that he was very hungry, had cut himself a sandwich and made some coffee. Wall stared at the ham in the sandwich as he talked.

"Head injuries caused by a blunt instrument, no doubt at all. I think Jolly was unconscious when pushed out of a car. I've drawn certain conclusions, Rollison."

"What are they?"

"Can't you guess?"

"I'm not in any mood for guessing," Rollison said savagely.

"You'd better be in a mood for looking at facts and drawing the right conclusions from them, or before long you'll end up in hospital," said Wall, mild as milk. "It's not like you to leave this to someone else. I don't like to see you do it."

After a long pause, Rollison relaxed, took a mouthful of lukewarm coffee, sat down in the chair where the snake had rustled the newspaper and said in a more relaxed tone: "Thanks. I needed that. Now let me see – the leg injuries are not serious, you say."

"No."

"The head injuries probably came first."

"Yes."

"Yet if he was unconscious why should they push him out of a car? Why take him away from here, for that matter? It pre-supposes they had some time to spare. And that pre-supposes that if they had wanted to kill him they could have done." He made himself add: "It's as easy to batter in an unconscious man's head as it is to injure his legs. Is that what you've been trying to make me see?"

Wall was smiling. He was rather like a chubbier and younger edition of Dr. Halliday, for he had bushy hair and eyebrows; but he was nothing like so craggy as Lady Gloria's doctor.

"That's right," he said. "They didn't want Jolly dead."

After a pause, Rollison replied softly: "Now I wonder if they wanted him to be an awful warning to me? If they didn't want him dead he couldn't have got a good look at them, and they wouldn't feel in any danger from him. So—"

He broke off.

"Now your mind's beginning to work again I'm going home, said Wall. "If I were you I'd go straight to bed. You look as if you'll have plenty to do in the morning."

Chapter Six

Homework

Rollison woke to unfamiliar sounds, and in the first few seconds was aware of hazy impressions of fear, a background of apprehension and anxiety. He lay absolutely still, listening intently. Suddenly recollection of the adders of the previous night came to his mind. He started, but stayed where he was, rigid. Next he was aware of the sounds again, footsteps in the kitchen much heavier than usual, voices, the banging of a kettle. He frowned. Jolly – *Jolly*.

He closed his eyes, remembering exactly what had happened. It was not long before he realised the explanation of the noises. His expression eased and his tension slackened. He knew that some of his friends and Jolly's friends had come to what they would call "the rescue," and the police must have admitted them. He glanced at his bedside clock, and saw that it was half past nine – not late, in view of the fact that he had been awake until half past four, thinking, tossing and turning.

He pushed back the bedclothes, then heard a nearer sound, at the door; the handle was turning. Hastily he pulled the clothes over him again and watched the door through his lashes. It opened, very slowly. He heard yet another sound, a curious kind of rustling and squeaking; this was the way in which Bill Ebbutt breathed. Ebbutt was the leader among these friends.

Ebbutt's hand appeared at the door and his nearly bald head above it. He was a huge man with several chins, rather like a turnip to look at. Long ago he had been one of the most reliable of British heavyweights and nowadays he trained more good fighters than anyone else in London. His asthmatic breathing made great difficulties for him in this work, but his Salvation Army wife made more.

He crept inside; and Ebbutt creeping, was a sight to see. He drew very close to the bed and stood looking down, and Rollison could see the concern on his face and the open affection which Ebbutt would never show if he thought Rollison could see it.

Ebbutt stretched out his hand and touched Rollison's shoulder gently. Rollison did not stir. Ebbutt touched him again, and whispered: "Mr. Ar, wake up."

Rollison stirred.

"Come on, Mr. Ar, if you lie there much longer the sun'll burn your eyes out! Mr. Ar! Wake up."

Rollison blinked, sighed, started; and went still, as if he had in fact just woken. Now Ebbutt gripped his shoulder with arthritic fingers which nevertheless had a grip of steel, and shook him as if he were a sack.

"Show a leg there, show a leg!" he roared. "Ten o'clock on a bright summer morning, if you don't show a leg you'll miss your cricket!"

Rollison opened his eyes and was now able to admit that he was awake.

"Hallo, Bill," he said, huskily. "Who let you in?"

"I'd like to see anyone try to keep me out," said Ebbutt bluffly. "The bloody cops. Got some good news for you, Mr. Ar. Jolly's had a good night. Slept like a top, he did. Nothing to worry about at all, I'm glad to say."

Rollison's heart leapt.

"That's wonderful," he said, and hitched himself up. Then he scowled. "But who told you? Have you been sitting up all night with him?"

"Gotta pal who's gotta sister who's gotta daughter who works at the Westminister, and she found out and reported," explained Ebbutt. It may well have taken him hours to ferret out the contact at the hospital, but Ebbutt always took infinite pains. "It's okay, Mr.

Ar, anyhow. Your pal Wall come on the line, too, to tell you that same thing. Not that I believe these pathologists, pathological cases themselves some of them. Want a cuppa first or going to have your bath?"

"A cuppa would be just right," said Rollison. "How many of your roughnecks have you brought along?"

"I'll thank you to be polite about my friends," reproved Ebbutt. He gave a vast, nearly toothless grin. "Six," he added, and turned and went out leaving the door ajar. He looked as if he would make the very walls shake, but he made hardly a sound and he still moved easily and well.

He returned five minutes later balancing a tray on one hand with the precision of a ballet dancer. He put it on Rollison's bedside table, and nearly knocked the clock off.

"Damn silly size, that table," he declared. "Want the papers?"

"What's the matter, Bill? Is your memory failing you?"

"All right, all right, I forgot 'em," said Ebbutt. He went out again and came back with the newspapers in one hand and the post in the other. "Just because I'm not as good as Jolly there's no need to snap me head off. How about that?" He opened one newspaper and thrust it in front of Rollison so that he had to squint to see it "'Orrible, if you ask me."

Rollison pushed the paper farther away, and saw a reasonably good photograph of himself. Next to it was one of a .22 bullet enlarged, and beneath these photographs of the murdered man and of the mystery girl.

"The bullet's 'orrible, I mean," Ebbutt said, and grinned again. "Well, I can't stay here gassing, I've got work to do if some people can slug abed all day."

He went to the door.

"What work, Bill?" inquired Rollison, sipping his tea.

"Homework, of course."

"The place is spick and span," protested Rollison.

"Well it won't be by the time you've messed around on your own for a bit, and I don't want Jolly coming home to find the place like a pigsty, do we?" Ebbutt grinned again. "As a matter of fact, Mr. Ar, we've turned the place inside out and upside down, on Mr. Grice's suggestion. He thought that if these perishers would use adders they might use smaller things, just as poisonous. Tarantulas, for instance, and scorpions. You know. So we've shifted every blasted thing. Nearly finished."

He went out happily.

Rollison finished two cups of tea and all of the stories about the murder and what had happened last night. They were accurate as far as they went, but all exaggerated the part he had played. Across one front page, for instance, ran the headline:

TOFF SAVES MYSTERY GIRL

Another smaller headline ran:

Hero Toff Saves Girl

The Times said:

> *The Hon. Richard Rollison, of 23g, Gresham Terrace, W.I., was able to fend off an attack made by an unknown assailant in Belsize Square last night. The attack was made on a young lady who appeared to be suffering from amnesia. Mr. Horace Wall ...*

Rollison pushed the papers to one side, drew on his dressing-gown and went into the bathroom. The glimpses he caught of the other rooms showed that the furniture had been put back roughly in the same position as it had been, but Jolly would have shuddered had he seen the state of the flat. There would be all too much time to put that right, Rollison reflected. He turned on his bath, hung up his dressing-gown, stripped and turned round, one leg poised to climb in. He saw a round dark-brown object swirling round in the water near the rush of water – and he stood as if mesmerised. He could see tiny eyes. He could see the way legs were hugging the body. He knew what it was. Ebbutt had mentioned the name earlier. He drew his leg back slowly and turned the tap off. As the water settled and calmed, the tarantula began to move about sluggishly, making experimental probings with its legs. Once it turned so that Rollison could see the mouth as well as the eyes. He waited there for what seemed a long time, and went out slowly. Two men were vacuuming the spare bedroom. Ebutt and another hefty were shifting a wardrobe from the wall of Rollison's room so that they could look behind it.

"Come and have a look at this, Bill," Rollison said quietly.

Ebbutt, impressed by his tone, put his end of the wardrobe down cautiously and went out with Rollison, leaving the other large, chunky man still clutching the wardrobe, which was resting on his foot.

"Yes," Grice said. "A tarantula."

"Did you see the obvious last night?" asked Rollison.

"It depends what you regard as obvious?"

"That we had to look for someone who not only handled deadly snakes quite confidently but knew what the effect of a bite would be."

"A naturalist, you mean – or a zoologist."

"That's right," said Rollison.

"It passed through my mind."

"When I saw that thing"—Rollison pointed to the furry body of the spider now on a sheet of white paper on Grice's desk—"I woke to the fact that we are dealing with someone who can handle these things – they don't scare him – and has access to them. It isn't the easiest thing in the world to get hold of an adder. To get two is really difficult but not impossible in England. To have access to a tarantula is a very different matter. We want a professional, a man who buys and sells or keeps these brutes as pets."

Grice echoed: "Pets."

"You know what I mean."

"Yes, and I hope you're right," Grice said, slowly. "It means that if we can narrow down the search to someone involved in this kind of interest we've a much better chance of getting results. The man who knows most about these things at the Yard is on holiday. I've asked Professor Slimm to come over. You know him don't you?"

Rollison said in a startled voice: "Sammy Slimm?"

"Yes."

Rollison did what he had not expected to do for some time: he gave a broad expansive grin.

"I certainly do," he admitted. "When we were at school together Sammy could let spiders run round his tongue. He used to give the rest of us the willies. But I thought he was in South America, bug-hunting."

"He's back with his bugs," Grice said. "He's been home for a week, and he says he's been working day and night to get all of his prizes indexed. He refused point-blank to come until I told him you were involved. What odd friends you have, Rolly."

Rollison laughed again.

"Sammy isn't odd," he declared. "He just has a peculiar ability to get on with spiders, snakes and other creepy-crawlies. The funny thing is, he hates flies. He—"

Grice's telephone bell rang.

He picked it up, listened and said. "Yes, send him along right away." He put down the receiver and went on to Rollison: "That was your friend Sammy. He'll be here in a couple of minutes. Let's go through what we've had in the reports this morning. On the man on the motor-scooter: negative. We traced him as far as Piccadilly Circus and then lost him. The dead man: still negative. The girl: negative. We've had a lot of reports saying that each has been recognised, but they've all been false." Grice was scanning a sheet of paper in his hand. "There's a half possibility that they landed at Dover from the Calais Ferry on Monday afternoon, but the ferry was so packed that no one can be sure. If they were our couple, the girl had dark hair – good job Lady Gloria spotted the dye or we would have been looking in the wrong place all the time. I've sent two men down to Dover to check, and I've asked the port police, customs officials and the immigration men to help. Then—"

"Anyone carrying snakes and tarantulas on board that ferry?" inquired Rollison.

"What?"

"Was there?"

"My dear chap—" Grice began. Then he broke off and raised his hands almost helplessly. "I see what you mean. Did anyone declare that he had such things, or could they have been smuggled through? It can't be as easy as that, but you've given me another idea, Rolly." He picked up the telephone and called *Information*. "I want a teleprint request to go to all air and sea ports for information about any individuals or parties who have entered the country recently with licence to bring in biological specimens such as snakes, spiders, monkeys …" He gave a list of about a dozen species, waited for the man to reply and rang off. He was smiling dourly at Rollison. "Good idea. We might pick something up from that. I've already sent out a request to all Home Counties, London and the main provincial forces asking for information about keepers of pet shops, private zoos and experimental laboratories."

There was a tap at the door.

"This will be your Sammy Slimm," he remarked, and called: "Come in."

The door opened, a grey-haired messenger said: "Professor Slimm, sir," and stood with the door wide open. On the instant, Sammy Slimm came in. But instead of beaming at Rollison, instead of speaking calmly to Grice, he strode in, ignored Rollison and declared in a squeaky voice: "I know him."

Grice said: "Know whom, Professor Slimm?"

Sammy turned to Rollison at last. He was a very tall, bony man, he had his hair cut very short in a crew cut, his nose was peeling after sunburn and his face and forehead were a mass of freckles.

"I know that chap," he announced. "That chap whose body they found on Hampstead Heath. Brilliant mind. Absolutely brilliant. Portuguese professor of biology. Renowned naturalist, of course. What worries me is, where's his daughter?"

Chapter Seven

Sammy Slimm

Grice made a slight movement of his right hand towards Rollison, who saw it out of the corner of his eye and knew that the Yard man wanted him to deal with Sammy for the time being. Sammy was now oblivious, it seemed, of everything except Rollison and the problem of the daughter of the Portuguese professor of biology. Eyes which Rollison remembered so well from the days of his youth, grey-green with a ring of gold which made them somehow like a bird's, caught reflected sunlight and took on a compelling brilliance.

"Sammy," said Rollison, "why didn't you tell us before?"

"Rolly," said Sammy Slimm, "why must you always evade a question?"

"Every newspaper in the country carried that man's photograph and yet you didn't come forward."

"What makes you think I read newspapers?"

"Why didn't you telephone the Yard as soon as you knew who the dead man was?" countered Rollison.

For a moment it looked as if Sammy would explode; but suddenly he gave a quick, expansive grin which made him look a little like an overgrown Frank Sinatra.

"First time I saw Estino's photograph was downstairs," he declared. "There's a pin-up in the entrance hall. As I told the Superintendent I've been so busy I haven't had time for the niceties of life, if you can call reading newspapers a nicety. First time I knew who the dead man was three minutes ago. I'd heard about the Hampstead murder, but that didn't ring a bell."

"No television?"

Sammy screwed up his face and looked vaguely like a disappointed frog.

"No television. If there happens to be a decent programme on, such as Deep In The Heart of Borneo or Relics of the Upper Amazon, I slip into my gardener's cottage. And there are no pictures on radio. Who killed him?"

"Who hated him?" asked Rollison.

"I dunno."

"When did you see him last?"

"Now let me see," said Sammy, screwing up his face again and becoming somewhat pensive. "Five weeks ago, in Aro – capital of Arodia. And a hell of a time it was. There'd been a terrible scrap up in the hills. What with one prince shooting it out with another prince, the United Nations tripping up all over the place and the Chinese and the Yanks spitting at each other the flora and fauna of the place didn't have a chance. Estino was out there looking for a Simi monkey up in the hill country which is half Laotian and half Siamese to Thai-ese if you want to be up to date, and wholly Arodian. Marta was with him. They'd two guides left and a couple of dogs and one mule and I offered to bring 'em back but Estino's a stubborn old—" Sammy stopped, frowned, now screwed up his eyes as if to shut out an unpleasant vision. "Well, he was. Damned shame. Got his murderer yet?"

"We want you to help us find him."

"Glad to," said Sammy, succinctly. Now he turned to Grice. "What about his daughter?"

Grice rounded his desk, sat down, opened a file and handed a photograph of the girl who had been found wandering in London's West End. Rollison held his breath as Sammy took it and studied it. Sammy, always unpredictable, did not speak for fully half a minute, and judging from his blank expression the photograph meant nothing to him. Then: "That's her."

"Sure?" asked Grice.

"If I say a thing I mean it."

"I'll vouch for that," put in Rollison. "Anything different about that photograph from what you remember?"

"Hair," answered Sammy promptly. "She's gone blonde. She was olive-black. I wish I could make you understand what it was like. Bloody hot day – steaming all over the damned place. We were in a patch of jungle and hardly knew the sun was anywhere about. Dark as a Stygian cave. I pushed aside some great big leaves and there she was coming towards me in a clearing, the sun shining on her. Yes, the *sun*. It was like coming upon an ancient or do I mean olden-day princess. That shiny black hair on that golden face and those blue eyes—*phhwee!* I forgot to mention that she wore a grass skirt and not much else. She didn't realise she was going to have visitors, of course, and all I had on was a pair of short pants and a pair of boots. I thought I'd come across an unknown tribe or one of these freak instances of a lost white baby cared for by kindly natives. We just stood staring at each other. She never told me what *she* thought at the moment of meeting. Then her father turned up and spoiled the illusion."

"And presumably she was covered in confusion."

"Who?"

"Marta."

"She wasn't covered in anything but the grass skirt," said Sammy. "Plus a grass scarf she threw across her shoulders in view of the presence of a strange male with peculiar ideas of what is proper. Or else who might get ideas. She's the most natural and nicest person I've ever met and can she cook! Even in that stinking patch of primeval forest she could cook. *Do* you know where she is?"

"Yes," said Grice.

"Thank God for that. I suppose"—Sammy hesitated—"she knows."

"About her father?"

"Do coppers always waste time on the obvious?" Sammy appealed to Rollison.

"Yes. They also like answers."

"Very well," said Sammy, thrusting his not very impressive chest out. "Does Marta know that her father was murdered? It must have been a terrible shock. She was devoted, absolutely devoted. Don't often find that kind of relationship these days. Estino told me about it. He'd done most of his work in Angola and Portuguese East Africa, spent most of his life there, and Marta was born in Angola. His wife died when she was ten or eleven, and he educated her, brought her up with the help of coal black nammies and things. He could speak English, French, Spanish, German, Dutch and his native Portuguese fluently – and so could Marta. They were up on African tribal languages, too. Maria's only companions in her childhood were the local children and whatever they did she did and whatever she did they did. The whole province venerated Estino, I gather – he didn't tell me that. Marta did. He was the local doctor, surgeon, father confessor, electrician, engineer, water diviner – the lot. And in return they brought him all the specimens of flora and fauna, alive or dead, that they could come across. That's why the museum in Lisbon had a few rarities which don't exist anywhere else in the civilised world. Then Estino got the itch to look for this monkey, and things weren't so good in Angola anyhow. I gathered from his daughter and a man I know in the Portuguese Embassy in London that Estino is—oh, hell, was—absolutely non-political. He simply couldn't take sides, but did anything he could for any human being who suffered. Eventually he left on that last trip." Sammy shook his head very slowly. "I wonder if he got it."

"Got what?" asked Grice.

"The Simi monkey he was after," Rollison answered. "I don't think it was ever announced, if he did."

"Who would announce it?" inquired Grice.

"If he ever returned to Portugal with it the Portuguese would have told that part of the cultural world which cares," Sammy Slimm asserted.

"Would it be worth anything?"

"It would be unique."

"Would it be worth anyone's while to murder a man to get the monkey?"

Sammy looked narrowly at Grice. "You have motive on the brain," he declared. "No, it would not. We seekers after the rare and the beautiful and particularly the anthropological specialists who are trying to find the missing link or links do not hate each other or envy each other or wish one another dead. The objectives of one are common to all. One discovery made by Estino or Tom, Dick and Harry is the pride, possession and progress of all of us – Russian and American and everyone in between. How can I help to find his murderer?"

Before Grice could answer and before Rollison could make any comment Sammy's expression changed again and he spoke in a different kind of voice, as if suddenly he felt acute pain. "Does Marta know?"

Rollison answered gently: "Yes, Sammy. At least, we think so. You see …"

As he talked he sat on the edge of Grice's desk. Grice sat in his chair, Sammy Slimm stood by the window with the sun shining on the back of his head and making the red glint; but it put his eyes in shadow. No telephone call came through and there were no interruptions. Sammy did not speak. He gave the impression at times that he was not even concentrating. Rollison's voice maintained its level tone, giving no emphasis, just flatly stating the facts. When he finished he stretched out for water from a carafe and glass on Grice's desk, poured and sipped. It seemed a long time before Sammy moved. Then all he did was place his hands together and rub them slowly; he had big, knuckly hands.

"How soon can I see her?" he asked at last.

"As soon as she comes round, and that will not be until this afternoon, at the earliest."

"She must have seen it happen," Sammy declared. "She must have. It would shock her beyond belief. If you knew how she worshipped that man—" He broke off, with a catch in his voice. "And someone tried to kill *her*."

"Yes."

Grice demurred. "There's one thing about the shooting last night you don't seem to have thought enough about, Rolly."

"What's that?"

"The man might have been after you."

"We've disregarded that one surely," Rollison insisted. "They tried to kill her, Sammy. Sammy—"

"Yes."

"Do you know of any motive that could possibly explain what's happened?"

"None at all," answered Sammy, quite promptly. "I've been thinking about that ever since I realised that the dead man was Estino. I've been over everything I know about him and everything he told me about, and I can't think of any motive at all. Something might click later." He drew a deep breath. "Marta will know, of course."

"If we can persuade her to talk."

"We'll get her to talk." Sammy said. "Or *I* will."

"That's fine," said Rollison, without arguing. "It can't be too soon for us. Have you seen this little joker?" He shifted his position and poked the dead body of the spider with his forefinger; it filled him with a sense of horror as it had at the moment when he had seen it whirling around in the bath.

'Tarantula," Sammy said after a cursory glance.

"Where is that kind of thing to be found in this country?"

"Hundreds of places although you may not realise it,' said Sammy. "And what's that?" He looked at the crushed remains of an adder contained in a cellophane bag, moved towards it, wrinkled his nose and went on: "Genus *Vipera,* north Europe's one and only lethal snake. Someone been after you with these?"

"Yes "

"Not Laotian, if that's what's in your mind. Not Far East, either. The spider's from the southern states or far Western of America, Mexico or South America. Someone got 'em from a zoo or whatnot, I should say."

"We want to find out which whatnot."

"Not my speciality," said Sammy. "Still I could make a few inquiries and find out whether any of my friends have had any of these jokers stolen lately. Where were they?"

Rollison explained.

"So you're looking for someone who can handle the things," said Sammy. "Anyone who can put a tarantula up a water faucet must know what he's doing. How was it held in?"

"By a piece of sellotape across the mouth of the tap. The tape was freed by the force of the water when the tap was turned full on."

"Smart," approved Sammy. "Well, let's see. The adders could be handled by an amateur, but in fact they seldom are. Most people hate the things. But that's only routine, isn't it? I can really help with Marta, I hope." He screwed up his eyes and asked before opening them again: "She isn't hurt, is she?"

"Not physically," Grice said.

Those green-ringed eyes opened.

"Nice distinction. My opinion of policemen is rising every minute." Sammy turned and looked out of the window. "As I've been prised away from my private zoo and my precious card index I might as well take it easy for a while. First time I've been to London with an hour or two to spare for a long time. Years. I never did like London, but I must say that you have one of the handsomest views of it. River looks good this morning, doesn't it?"

"Like to have a trip up river with one of our launches?" asked Grice.

"V.I.P. treatment?"

"Yes."

"Please."

"I'll fix it." Grice said. "How about you, Rolly?"

"No, thanks," Rollison said "I'll be at the Marigold Club at two o'clock. If Sammy will meet me there we'll go and see Marta as soon as she's come round and can have visitors. It's hard to believe, but the sight of his ugly mug might possibly help her."

After a pause, Sammy said softly: "Rolly."

"Yes?"

"Do me a favour."

"Of course."

"Don't joke about Marta Estino," Sammy said. "And keep me away from the swine who's done this to her. I'd like to choke the life out of him."

His hands were clasped together; big, strong hands.

Chapter Eight

Help

Marta was awake.

First a nurse who was also a policewoman, then Maggie, then Lady Gloria all looked in on her and tried to make her speak but, they reported, she simply lay on her back and stared at the ceiling as if she had taken a vow of silence. Rollison went with Sammy to the room and stepped inside. It was small but very charming, bright with green and yellow motifs on the wallpaper and on the furniture, a room that a woman could love and a girl delight in. The bed was behind the door. Rollison glanced at the girl and did not know whether she knew he was there or not. He stepped to the foot of the bed and stood there smiling.

"Hallo," he said.

She did not move her head, but looked at him; it made it seem as if her eyes were closed.

"How are you feeling?"

She didn't answer.

"I've brought a friend to see you," Rollison said.

She did not speak or look at the door, but continued to look at him through her lashes.

"A good friend," added Rollison. He glanced at the open door and Sammy advanced. He had known Sammy for so long, but had never seen him anything like he was now. The only word was nervous. His hands were clasped in that characteristic fashion of his. He kept moistening his lips.

His face was twisted into a kind of smile which lacked all the spontaneous naturalness which was in the man himself. He took a long step forward, hesitated and shuffled another. He looked down at her, but she did not turn her head towards him. He screwed up his eyes and drew a deep breath. It was easy to believe that he was fighting a lone battle, telling himself not to be a fool. He went closer to the bed.

"Hallo, Marta," he said and added some words in Portuguese.

Rollison watching with a tension which was strange to him, saw her eyes open wider. She stared at the ceiling, but except for that terror when she had crouched by the car last night, this was the first time he had seen any kind of emotion on her face.

"It's been a long time," Sammy said. He shifted his position, stood close to the bed and stared down at her. His tension seemed to ease, and Rollison saw the deep concern that was in his eyes, the anxiety, almost the dread. His voice went up. "Marta, it's me. Sammy."

She turned her head. Her eyes opened wide and seemed to grow huge and brilliant. She rose from her pillow, supporting herself with her elbows, and she looked into Sammy Slimm's eyes, her lips parted, her whole face aglow.

"Sammy!" she said in a husky voice. "Oh, Sammy!"

"How long do you propose to leave them together?" inquired Lady Gloria.

"Do you think it's mildly improper?" inquired Rollison.

"Don't talk nonsense. I think that the meeting might be too intense, and that she might have a sharp reaction from it. I think we should go in."

"They've only been there for twenty minutes," said Maggie Lister, half protesting.

"I'll go in," volunteered Rollison.

"I think you should be satisfied with the progress you have made with her," his aunt said, firmly. "I feel sure it would be a mistake to ask too many questions at this stage. Above everything else I am sure that we should see that she doesn't relapse at all. Can I trust you, Richard?"

"You worry too much, Glory," Rollison told her, and turned towards the door of the little bedroom.

It opened before he touched the handle and Sammy Slimm came out. He closed the door behind him firmly and stood with his back to it – with his hand at the handle, as if determined to make sure that no one could get past. He looked defiantly at Rollison, but ignored the others with that peculiar faculty he had of dealing with only one person at a time.

"She's asleep," he announced. "Natural sleep. She mustn't be disturbed."

"That's good," said Rollison.

"Don't try to fool me, Rolly."

"I'm not fooling," Rollison assured him. "The police will want a nurse to sit in the room with her, but she won't be asked any questions and won't be disturbed until she wakes of her own accord."

Sammy said doubtfully: "I suppose that will be all right." He looked at the police nurse, a tall, middle-aged woman with iron-grey hair. "That a promise?"

"Yes, sir."

"Go in very quietly," pleaded Sammy.

"Did she say anything, sir?"

"Nothing that matters."

"Did she say anything at all?"

"Yes," said Sammy. He gave a curious little twitching smile. "She said that she was glad to see me. She said that it had been horrible. She said that she knew her father was dead. And then she started to cry. In the middle of her crying she fell asleep."

"That's most unusual," remarked the nurse.

"Well, it happened."

"Oh, I'm not questioning you, sir, but it is most unusual." The nurse went past Sammy as if defying him to stop her, and went inside. She looked round the door, seemed satisfied and closed the door. Out on the landing it was quite shadowy.

Sammy thrust past Rollison and stood in front of Lady Gloria.

"I can't tell you how grateful I am, nor how grateful Marta will be, Lady Gloria. Thank you very, very much." He took her right hand in both of his and pressed. "You always were much more than Rolly deserved, you know. You were my favourite other boy's visiting aunt. Do you remember boxing my ears when I put some spiders in the teacup and stood a saucer on top of it? The maid screamed and the housemaster's tea party was nearly ruined."

"I remember very well," said Lady Gloria. "I trust you have grown out of that kind of practical joke."

"Spiders aren't a joking matter with me any longer!" Sammy assured her. "And scaring the wits out of people no longer appeals to me, either."

Rollison noticed that his hands were tighter even as they clasped Lady Gloria's; another woman might well have shown some sign of pain. She did not.

"It's very good to see you again, even if we have to mourn a mutual failure."

"I don't quite understand you," said Lady Gloria gently.

"Well, look what a mess your once favourite nephew has made of his life!"

It was a long time since Rollison had seen his aunt laugh so much. Even when Sammy had gone for a hurried trip back to his creepy-crawlies – he was to be at Rollison's flat by eight o'clock that night – she kept chuckling to herself. She was so delighted with Sammy Slimm, in fact, that Rollison did not confide his private anxiety to her. It was a time when he missed Jolly very much indeed, for he could talk to Jolly as to a second self, whereas he could not always talk freely to Grice or anyone else.

He left Old Glory to her dreams of boxing Sammy's ears and yesteryear, and went along to the little office where Maggie Lister worked. This was at the back, overlooking a small courtyard, and the sun was on the other side of the house. The room struck cool; on cold days it was icy. Maggie was a competent woman in her late forties, a little mannish and perhaps too efficient at times, but with a remarkable capacity for human kindness and for the understanding of human weaknesses. She had been in the Probationer Service for years, and had come here when Lady Gloria had needed someone who could take over the Marigold Club. Now she put down her pen and turned in her swivel chair to Rollison.

"You're troubled about something, aren't you?"

"Yes, Maggie. Can you get the nurse out of Marta's room for ten minutes?"

"Yes. But she'll want me to stay with the patient."

"That's reasonable," said Rollison. "I'll need you, too." He lit a cigarette and stared at the mellow red brick of the house across the courtyard. "Ten minutes?"

"Meet me up there," said Maggie. It was like her not to ask questions. She went out, tweed skirt whirling about sturdy web-stockinged legs. Ten minutes later Rollison stepped into the Portuguese girl's room again. He closed the door and Maggie Lister asked: "What do you expect to find?"

"A puncture," Rollison answered.

"A punc—" Maggie echoed, and then her face paled. "Oh. I see." She turned to Marta, who lay on her back and seemed more unconscious than asleep. She turned back the sheet from her shoulders, and Rollison examined one beautifully rounded arm and shoulder, while Maggie examined the other; they found no blemish except the scratch and bruise from the car the previous night. Yet she did not react at all, or move, and she allowed Maggie to push her about and move her without taking the slightest notice. "Let's look at her back," said Maggie. She supported the girl, breast to breast, and slipped a short-sleeved nightdress off her shoulders. Her back was beautiful and satiny.

"Ah!" exclaimed Rollison.

There, in the fullness of the flesh beneath the shoulder blade was a tiny red mark, the kind that would be made by a needle. Maggie examined it closer as Rollison took out a pocket magnifying glass to make quite sure that he was right.

"It's a recent one," Maggie said, rather huskily. "In the past hour I would say."

"You think Mr. Slimm did this?"

"Professor Slimm. Yes, I do. That's why he made such a point of telling us she mustn't be disturbed."

Maggie said in a strained voice: "But why should he want to put her to sleep again?"

"Possibly to make sure she cannot talk," suggested Rollison. "Possibly—" he broke off. "There's another, even more important question, though. Why did he carry a hypodermic syringe loaded with whatever he pumped into her?" Rollison watched as Maggie slipped the nightdress on again, hardly noticing the gentle curves of the girl's breasts, and when she was lying on her back he raised one eyelid.

"Pinpoint," he said. "Morphine."

"Has the Professor any right to have morphine in his possession?"

"Oh, yes. He uses the stuff a lot to keep his specimens quiet, sometimes it's very necessary," Rollison said. "But I wouldn't expect him to keep a syringeful of it in his pocket, would you? I wonder why he lied?"

"Lied about what?"

Rollison said: "Maggie dear, I don't want to involve you too much. Keep this to yourself, won't you – if Lady Gloria had an inkling she would be worried out of her mind."

"I think you underrate Lady Gloria," said Maggie shrewdly. "But it would worry her a bit, of course. Of course I'll keep it to myself. You do realise that the nurse might also have found out what's happened, don't you?"

"It's not likely," Rollison said.

"Why not?"

"She hasn't telephoned the Yard, and if she had guessed what happened she would have wanted to report at once. She would have asked you to take over while she powdered her nose and slipped in the call. She might wake up to it later, but she's more likely to be convinced that this is a secondary effect of the sedation. Maggie, be very careful here, won't you?"

Maggie said: "I wish I knew what you meant."

"You do know. You remember what happened at my flat, don't you? Watch everything that comes in – groceries, greengroceries, laundry – anything. Especially watch anything that comes up to this room, such as flowers or fruit or even boxes of chocolates."

After a pause, Maggie said: "I think I'm very scared. You mean that tarantulas or other beastly things could be hidden in a gift of flowers or fruit?"

"Yes."

Maggie shivered.

"I'll be careful," she said. "But surely the police will examine everything that comes in."

"Provided you double-check, everything will be all right," Rollison said, almost too glibly. He gripped Maggie's hand. "Thanks, Maggie. I'll let you off this hook just as soon as I can."

"I'm sure you will," Maggie said. "Did you know that she is left-handed, by the way? I know you like that kind of tit-bit."

It didn't help, Rollison knew; but it was gratifying to be proved right.

"Thanks, Maggie," he said. "You never know when that kind of thing might come in useful."

He knew that when he left, half an hour afterwards, Maggie watched him closely. He also knew that she felt an affection towards him which she had to keep under strict control. It would never become a problem and it would enable him always to be sure of her absolute loyalty, but the Maggies of this world were the old maids who should have been wives and mothers.

Rollison did not think much about Maggie once he was out of the Marigold Club, but switched to the new and absorbing problem of Sammy Slimm.

Just what was Sammy up to?

How was it that Grice had got in touch with him? If he, Sammy, had made the first approach it might be easier to understand. Now it was so much like the more unbelievable kind of coincidence. Sammy had known Estino, Sammy professed to be in love with Estino's daughter, Sammy came to the Yard prepared to be able to put her to sleep.

Had he come expecting to be taken to the girl?

This wasn't a possibility to discuss with Grice yet Rollison decided, and again he wished that he could talk to Jolly.

He drove in his silver-grey Bentley to the Westminster Hospital, where parking space was found for him because he was on one of the Appeals Committees which still flourished for those services of the hospital which were not paid for by the National Health Service. Porters, nurses, matrons, doctors, were all glad to see him, all full of assurances about his man – and there in a private ward with the evening sun shining in at the top of the window was Jolly, actually conscious, his bandaged head raised a little on his pillow, a cage over his legs.

Rollison's heart leapt.

"Jolly, this is wonderful!"

"I am very glad that you have no need to worry unduly, sir," said Jolly in a relaxed voice. "I have told the police stenographer who was waiting for me to come round that I opened the door to a straightforward ring and something quite noxious was squirted into my face from an insect spray, I think. I did not catch even a glimpse of the assailant's face, sir, and I have no recollection of what happened after receiving the blow on the head. I wish very much that I could help more."

"I wish you could forget it," Rollison said. "Bill Ebbutt has rallied round, everyone's spoiling me as they always do and they're all worried about their friend Jolly. I can tell them that they needn't be. Just one little thing, Jolly."

"Yes, sir?"

"What kind of spray was it? Do you remember?"

"Oh, a household insect spray of some make," Jolly answered. "I'm quite positive of that."

Chapter Nine

Pet Shop

Bill Ebbutt had gone, leaving only one of his men, a small and wizened and highly domesticated ex-lightweight whose name was Percy Wrightson. Percy stood in for Jolly from time to time, and was usually called in to help with spring cleaning and for special events. Consequently he knew the Gresham Terrace flat nearly as well as Jolly, and could be relied on to do everything that was necessary; even to cook simple meals.

Rollison looked about the flat, seeing that everything had indeed been moved, and most of the pictures and ornaments were out of position, but at least he felt that there was no danger that he might shift a cushion and be stung or bitten.

There was a message from Grice, which said simply: *"Negative reports from al. airports and sea ports."*

"And there was a call from a man who just asked for you and when I said you weren't in he rang off. Rude so-and-so," observed Percy, who had a long, wriggly nose which was always shiny red, so giving the false impression that he imbibed his liquor too freely, "He just rang off, Mr. Ar."

That was what the caller of the previous night had done.

"It's the way he'd been brought up," said Rollison earnestly. "How many newspapers have called?"

"Seven, *and* the Independent tee-vee people. They said it would be too late this afternoon. I told everyone else you wouldn't be back until late tonight, that's why you're getting a breathing space, I dare say."

"You have genius," Rollison declared. "Jolly always said that you were the only man who ever made him think that his job was in jeopardy."

"Did he, then?" Percy was deeply pleased. "Well I never. Shouldn't have thought it. I'll tell you what, if I posh up me voice a bit for when he gets back we'll really give him a shock, won't we? If I say Mr. Rawlisson instead of Mr. Ar, I mean. That kind of caper. Mr. Rawlisson." Percy was now delighted, "All I want is a bit of practice."

"You keep at it," urged Rollison. "I'm going over to see Bill Ebbutt. If anyone rings up give them the same answer, will you? Except to Professor Slimm. He's due here at eight o'clock and will probably be hungry. If he's back before 1 am, feed him well and try to make him patient."

"Okay," said Percy. "I mean very gude, Mr. *Raw-lis*-son."

He sounded as if he were overjoyed.

Rollison took the Bentley, which was attracting no attention in Mayfair where such cars were not rare, and drove towards the East End. He took side streets across to the Embankment before driving fast to Blackfriars Bridge. He had never seen the Thames looking more brilliant nor so many gaily coloured awnings on the boats. London seemed to be revelling in a heat wave which was tempered all the time by a soft breeze. Girls in sleeveless blouses kept reminding him of Marta Estino, and what Sammy had done. Men carrying their coats reminded him of Sammy, who had always carried his coat slung over his shoulder, like many of these. Traffic policemen looked hot, taxi-drivers looked sticky, Blackfriars Bridge looked dirty, but the Bank of England seemed as solid and safe as the adage about it. The narrow streets of the City of London seemed

to capture and increase the heat; it was positively sizzling here. At Aldgate Pump, the landmark which divided the City from the East End, he slowed down because of the bottleneck. It might take twenty minutes to get from here to the fork junction of Whitechapel and Mile End road, but after that it would be only a question of a few minutes' drive to the Blue Dog, the pub where Ebbutt had lived for many years and behind which stood his gymnasium. Both windows of the car were down, and the smell of diesel fumes and exhaust from petrol made Rollison wrinkle his nose. That reminded him of Sammy again. What was Sammy up to? Why—

Something passed in front of his eyes, inside the car. It was small and dark. He started. He was crawling at about five miles an hour and the flinch of alarm caused no harm. It was as if a big fly had flown in at the open window. He glanced down at the seat beside him and saw what it was; but it wasn't a fly or a wasp, it was a scorpion. He was quite sure about it. It lay still, as if stunned by the fall, but might not stay like that for long. It was within a few inches of him. He knew how swiftly the venomous insects could move, and how painful, if not fatal, their bite could be.

The traffic surrounded and trapped him, the sun beat down, the rumble and the growl of engines, the tapping of high heels and the thump of men walking, all these familiar sights and sounds were about him – and the little black insect crouched there. He could not be sure whether it was stunned, or simply wary. Traffic began to move faster. He dared not do anything which would make him take his eyes off the scorpion for long, but the slow-moving stream of traffic made it easy to keep going and to keep on glancing down.

He slid his left hand into his pocket and took out the gold cigarette case which was badly scratched at one corner after he had thrown it last night. He pressed it open. A cigarette fell out, with a shower of tobacco shreds. He turned it upside down, wide open.

A motor-scooter rasped along. Rollison turned his head towards it remembering the man of the previous night, but the rider was a pretty young girl with a white helmet on, seeing a gap in the traffic and taking advantage of it. A lad whistled after her. They were close to Aldgate now.

The scorpion stirred, a little dart of movement nearer Rollison.

Slowly and deliberately Rollison lowered the cigarette case, then let it fall. It covered the scorpion completely. He brought his left hand down on the case, grinding and grinding into the seat. The traffic moved faster, but he was hardly moving at all and the cars behind began to hoot him. He took his hand away from the case, moistened his parched lips and accelerated a little. He kept glancing down, but nothing moved.

When he reached the fork of the two main roads he turned to the right, and at the first opportunity turned right again and pulled up. He was sweating freely, and it wasn't because of the heat. Two boys, aged ten or eleven, came rushing across the road to see the car, and stood making comments.

"That's a Jaguar."

"Don't be daft, it's a Bentley."

"It's one of the new Jags, I tell you."

"It's a Rolls-Bentley!"

"Let's ask the chap." They drew nearer to Rollison, wide-eyed, long-haired, eager kids. "Say, mister—" The speaker broke off.

Rollison was staring down at the seat and the mess that the cigarette case had made of the scorpion. It would be a long time before he looked down at that seat without remembering what had happened in the last few minutes, but at least there was no more danger at this moment.

There might be in the next moment, in the next minute or the next hour. Someone passing by had tossed that creature in, and there was no telling where attacks might stop. He wiped his forehead with a snow-white handkerchief as the boys gathered confidence and asked: "Say, mister, what car is this?"

"Eh?"

"What car?"

"Car? Oh – this car." Rollison forced a smile. "It's a Bentley Continental."

"See!" the other lad jeered. "*I* knew it was a Bentley. Fancy you calling it a Jag."

Rollison got out of the car as they rushed off, attracted by an ice-cream van which turned into the street, its call bell ringing. He closed the windows, leaving an inch or two open at the top of the front ones for the air to get in. Then he changed his mind and pressed the automatic button to close them completely; that way he could make sure that nothing deadly was put inside the car. It wasn't possible to get at the engine from the outside, either.

He was within ten minutes' walk of the Blue Dog, but he could take twice as long if he went another way round. He went the long way. The narrow East End streets were very hot, the big new blocks of flats looked as if they were airy, though. Every window, high and low, every front door and every side door was open, to let in the longed-for breeze. It must be five degrees hotter here than by the river.

At every corner he took notice, but no one appeared to follow. By the time he got within sight of Ebbutt's pub he was quite sure that no one had followed him. It was half past five, a kind of siesta hour, before the Blue Dog opened and before the spare-time boxers who were managed by Bill Ebbutt began their work at the gymnasium. This was a big wooden structure on a plot of land behind the pub. It had been destroyed by a mob of hooligans some years ago, but soon rebuilt, so that now it looked fresh and new. The double doors were open and the interior looked dark and cool. With any luck Ebbutt would be sitting at his little partitioned office in a corner, labouring over accounts or correspondence.

Rollison, so sure that he had not been followed, stepped in. The momentary transition from bright sunlight to dark shade almost blinded him. He heard a rustle of movement, but it did not cause him any alarm until he saw a man rushing at him, one arm thrust forward, the other upraised and a weapon in it.

Rollison had no time to shout, hardly time to move, but he saw the man's left hand thrust forward and he sensed what was coming because of what Jolly had told him. He flung himself to one side and closed his eyes. He caught a whiff of a sickly odour – the stench of an insecticide spray – and went staggering, but at least he had not taken the cloud of beastly stuff full in the face. He felt a heavy blow on his shoulder – at least it missed his head. Instead of trying to save himself he dived forward, and as he reached the ground he swung round on his back and kicked out. He caught his assailant on the shin, heard a hiss of pain, felt savage anger and kicked out again. This time, more by luck than judgement, he caught the man on the knee-cap. That brought a squeal and a gasp.

The attacker fell helplessly across Rollison's legs, and his head was close to Rollison's right hand. Rollison spread his fingers and clutched the bare head and thrust it down into the sawdust which covered the wooden floor. The impulse to grind this man's face as he had ground the scorpion was almost irresistible, but after a moment he drew his hand back, pulled himself free and began to get up. The other man was lying motionless; probably he had banged his head when falling. Watching him warily. Rollison rose to his feet. The man twitched. Rollison backed away out of reach of outflung arm or leg and took in deep breaths.

He called: "You there, Bill?"

There was no answer. He glanced across to the door of the partitioned office where he had felt sure that Ebbutt would be, but there was no sign of him. The man here groaned. Rollison called again: "Bill."

As he called, footsteps sounded on the path leading to the double doors, quick and light; possibly help for the man on the ground. Rollison bent down and picked up an Indian club which his assailant had wielded, backed into a position from which he could bring the club down on the head of anyone who threatened danger. He saw a diminutive man in a pale blue T-shirt and a pair of khaki shorts run into the gymnasium, knees bobbing up and down like a prancing horse, elbows tucked into his side. He sped in and marked time, still with that prancing movement, until he became aware of the man on the floor.

He stood at attention.

"Strewth," he gasped.

"Hallo, Willie," Rollison said in a voice which sounded unfamiliar. "You're just the man I needed. Go over and see if Bill's in his office, will you? And if he isn't, go and find him."

"Straight away," said the man named Willie. He started off, legs working like pistons. He was a little simple-minded and saw himself as the world's great fly-weight. Ebbutt encouraged him to hope provided he always kept in training. That way he stayed happy. There was something pathetic about the little man as he pranced across to the office.

Rollison knew that the man on the floor was coming round and would soon try to escape. At the same time he knew that there was a very real risk that Ebbutt was in the office, badly injured.

Chapter Ten

The Cellar

As Willie reached the office and the man on the floor started to get up, two more men came briskly along the path to the gymnasium. They stepped inside and stopped short at sight of Rollison. They were old friends of Ebbutt, physical training instructors ahead of time for their evening's work. They knew Rollison well – one of them, in fact was Percy Wrightson's brother-in-law.

"Having a bit of a barney, Mr. Ar?" one asked.

"Just a bit," said Rollison. "This chap tried to crack my skull, and he may have had a go at Bill's too. Make sure he doesn't get away, will you?"

Each man was larger than the prisoner, who was now on one knee and staring at them fearfully.

"If he puts his hand to his pocket, tread on his fingers," Rollison said. "He might carry some nasty little surprises in those pockets."

"He'd better not put no hand nowhere," the speaker said menacingly.

Willie appeared at the office door, marking time with intense evidence of concern and beckoning Rollison, who went slowly towards him. The fall had shaken him but the fact that someone had guessed where he was corning and had lain in wait for him was the greater shock. Willie beckoned more furiously. Anxiety for Ebbutt made Rollison run the last few yards. Willie did a mark-time turn about and went inside, then stopped his prancing.

Ebbutt was squeezed in a corner, behind a tall stool he used for his desk work. A patch of sticking plaster smothered his mouth and chin and he could breathe only through his nose. For any asthmatic that was a dangerous handicap. He was struggling for breath and tears were streaming down his eyes. Rollison pushed past Willie. There was no time for gentleness, so he bent over Ebbutt, picked at a corner of the plaster until he could get a grip then ripped it off. Ebbutt gave a gasping kind of squeal. His breathing became a series of great gulps, and for a few seconds it looked as if he would choke. Rollison pulled him round and supported him so that he had more freedom of movement for his chest. The great body was shuddering with the effort. Ebbutt's heart had threatened to crack on him more than once, and he was under medical orders not to exert himself. There was a frightening risk that this might bring on a seizure.

Gradually, his breathing quietened. He tried to mutter something.

"Chair outside, Willie," Rollison said.

Willie hurried out. Rollison helped Ebbutt to his feet and supported him out of the little office towards a back door. Out here were some wooden garden chairs in which Ebbutt and some of the others sat in the sun occasionally. Willie was pushing one forward. Rollison helped Ebbutt to sit in it.

"Go and get some brandy, Willie, please."

"Brandy," echoed Willie. He pranced back into the gymnasium.

"You'll be all right, Bill," Rollison said. "And we've got the man. He won't do that again in a hurry."

"Caught me—by surprise," gasped Ebbutt.

"I'll bet he did. Don't talk yet."

Willie and one of the other men appeared, and reported that more men had arrived. They told Rollison that the prisoner was under strong guard. Willie had a brandy flask, kept handy in case someone was knocked out during a bout in one of the gymnasium's two rings, and Rollison gave Ebbutt a sip. Already the big man's colour was better, and it looked as if he might not have a bad reaction after all.

By now a little group of men surrounded him. This narrow open space was between the gymnasium and the wall of the Blue Dog, a seven-foot-high wall beyond which was the delivery area of the pub and the back of the public house itself. The upper windows of the Blue Dog overlooked this spot, and all the windows were wide open, but no one appeared and no one seemed to have realised that there was cause for alarm.

Ebbutt reached the stage where he would not be put off talking.

"I heard a movement in the gym, but thought nothing of it. I'm always getting salesmen and suchlike coming at all times of the day. Nothing to get alarmed about. This chap tapped on the door so I said come in, but before I could so much as turn round he'd squirted some stinking stuff in my eyes. The next I knew he'd conked me one, and when I come round there was I squashed in the corner like you found me. What's it all about, Mr. Ar?"

'The job we're working on," said Rollison. "Bill, can I borrow your number 3 cellar?"

"Eh? Oh!" Ebbutt, still a little dazed, smiled for the first time since he had come round. "Oh, sure. I get you. Number 3 cellar. Lemme get the keys for you." He went to his desk and drew out a huge bunch of keys, ran through them, selected two and took them off a big brass ring. "You wouldn't want to tell me why you want the cellar, would you?"

"Not yet, Bill," said Rollison, and winked.

"You're a one, you are," Ebbutt said, and was caught by a furious spasm of wheezing.

Two of the others frog-marched the prisoner across the gymnasium and out into the open space, while Rollison unlocked the door leading to the loading yard. The big double hatch doors leading to the cellar were closed. Ready hands opened them. A big shiny chute for beer barrels and crates led to the bowels of the cellar, and by its side was a small iron ladder, which Ebbutt himself used.

"I'll go down," Rollison said. "Push him after me, will you?"

The prisoner had not said a word, and even now he only tightened his lips. Rollison went backwards down the ladder and reached the foot. The cellar was rich with the redolence of beer and filled with huge barrels and stacked high with crates. He switched on two lights, and as he did so shadowy figures weaved about at the open hatch. Next moment he saw the prisoner thrust feet forward on the chute and two men giving him a shove. The man hurtled down, crying out in fear as he did so. His legs hit the cement floor and he cried out again, then pitched to one side. He lay gasping, his legs doubled up; the fact that he had so much movement in them proved that he was not seriously hurt.

Someone called: *"Want any help, Mr. Ar?"*

"Later," called Rollison.

He stepped to the prisoner, who tried to press away from him but could not. He gripped the man's coat collar and yanked him to a sitting position, then dragged him across the cellar and along a passage with wine bins on either side; more wine was drunk in London's East End than most people realised. At the end of this passage was a door marked *"3"* in white. Rollison used the larger of the two keys, unlocked the door and kicked it open, and pushed the prisoner inside. He followed him and switched on the light.

They blinked in the sudden brightness.

Number 3 cellar was quite small. Against one wall were bins containing champagne and against another bins containing liqueurs and cognacs. Dust turned the bottles grey and smothered the shelves. The third wall had a bench running alongside it, for this had once been used as a workshop. Now a few tools were stuck in a rack, there were several bottles with candles stuck in them and wax thick on the necks and shoulders, as well as some coils or rope used for securing loads to trolleys and trucks.

Rollison had not said a single word to his prisoner. Now he put a hammer-lock on the man and thrust him forward towards the far corner with the bench on one side and the bins on the other. Big rings were fastened to the bins so that ropes could be slung across them to prevent theft. Rollison thrust the prisoner's right hand through one of these rings and the prisoner tried to snatch himself free. Rollison slapped the side of his head savagely. The man went slack. Rollison looped a piece of rope round the man's wrist and the ring, so that he was captive.

Then Rollison stepped back.

This was the man who had fired at Marta outside the Marigold Club; he was quite sure. The rather odd-shaped nose, almost certain a result of a break in his youth, made the profile quite unmistakable. He wore the same light-brown suit, too, and the cut of his dark hair was familiar.

He stood gulping, staring at Rollison.

Rollison said: "I can call the police and you will go to prison for at least five years. Do you realise that?"

The man didn't speak.

"Or you can tell me who you work for, and you can stay here until the case is finished and Estino's murderer caught. Then you can go – provided you're not Estino's murderer."

"*I am not!*" the man cried.

The way he uttered the words showed how taut his nerves were. The accent made it clear that he was as English as Rollison, in spite of his southern European appearance. He was sweating, although it was very cool down here.

"Did you put the snakes and the spiders in my flat?"

"No. No, I didn't!"

"How do I know you're not lying?"

"I can't handle the things. They wanted me to once, but I can't handle them. I hate spiders!"

"That's something we can prove," said Rollison, softly. "And it's something I will prove as soon as it's necessary. What's your name?"

"Max – Max Cato."

"That had better be true, too. Who sent you to kill Marta Estino?"

"I—I wasn't sent to kill her. I—I had to frighten her, that was all."

"Who sent you?"

Cato licked his lips. "I can't tell you."

"Why not?"

"They'd kill me!"

"I see," said Rollison softly. "You're more frightened of them than of me." He drew closer, thrust his hands into the man's pockets and found a wallet inside. The wallet had twenty-odd pound notes and a few ten-shilling notes, but that was all – there was no driving licence, nothing to indicate his identity. Rollison went through his other pockets and found many oddments, bus tickets, a handkerchief, keys, a comb and loose change, but again there was nothing to show his identity.

"You take care, I'll say that for you," he said. "I'll ask you once more: who do you work for?"

The man licked his lips, but didn't speak.

"All right," said Rollison. He turned and went out, reached the end of the passage and was not at all surprised to find Ebbutt there with another man named Mick Parks. Ebbutt's lips looked sore and there were smears of blood where the adhesive tape had broken the skin when it had been torn away, but he seemed to be almost himself again. "Hallo, Bill," said Rollison. "Come a bit nearer number 3 and just say 'yes' when I ask you questions, will you? You too, Micky."

"Trust me," said Parks.

"Not talking, ain't he?" remarked Ebbutt. "Gimme ten minutes and the thick end of a rope and I'll loosen his tongue, Mr. Ar."

"We may have to try it," said Rollison, "but think how unlawful it would be!" He winked as he went along the passage with the bins on either side and stopped so that everything they said could be heard, but they could not be seen by the prisoner. "Bill, you know Ziggy Pinker, who runs that pet shop?"

"Sure I know Ziggy."

"Does he still keep those snakes of his?"

"Does he keep—" began Ebbutt, and then he realised what Rollison was getting at, and his tone changed. "Oh, them adders. Cor bless you, lets them run all over his face, Ziggy does. Why? Say, Mr. Ar, you're not suggesting that *Ziggy* had anything to do with the trouble at your flat. Not *Ziggy*. He wouldn't have allowed anyone to—"

"I just want to reverse the trick that was tried on me," said Rollison. "How many snakes does he keep, do you know?"

Ebbutt was very quick on the ball.

"About a dozen, I s'pose. Amazing how many people keep snakes as pets, you'd never believe it, would you?

Says they're ever so friendly, Ziggy does. There's one thing I don't agree with him about though. I think he ought to draw their fangs so that they're harmless, but he says that it doesn't matter how poisonous a snake is it won't do its master any harm. He's a real snake fancier, Ziggy is."

"Can you get him to bring half a dozen of his little pets here, Bill?"

"*Here?*"

"To keep your new friend company."

Ebbutt said, in a matter-of-fact voice: "Well, I dunno. Ziggy's a businessman, you know. He might hire them out, but he'd probably want you to buy them. I wonder how much snakes cost."

"That's all right," said Rollison. "They can't cost too much, and—"

He broke off, at a sound from the cellar beyond, paused, and went on: "I don't mind within reason what this job costs, but I'm going to make that man talk. So get hold of Ziggy, will you?"

"Right away, Mr. Ar."

"*Rollison!*" called the prisoner in a gasping voice. "I'll tell you all I know. Don't send for those snakes, I'll tell you."

Ebbutt gave a huge wink, and Micky Parks clapped his hands together explosively. Rollison paused, and then went back into Cellar 3.

Chapter Eleven

Zoo

"I tell you it's the truth," Max Cato said desperately. "He paid me five hundred pounds to come and shoot Marta Estino. I lied to you before, he *did* want me to kill her. I was going to murder her. I've worked for him before, so I couldn't refuse."

"Did you shoot Estino?"

"No!"

"Were you there when he was shot?"

"No, I wasn't there. But I—I helped to move him away from where he was killed. I drove the car that took him to Hampstead Heath. That's all I know about it. If you find any marks from my shoes there that's the explanation. I had nothing to do with his murder." The man's voice was quivering.

"I hope that's the truth too," Rollison said. "And the name of your employer is Bell, you say."

"Yes, that's right, Matheson Bell. He supplies snakes and lizards and spiders to zoos all over Europe. He's one of these people who go overseas exploring and looking for rare animals and plants. He handles all kinds of creatures, but mostly snakes and spiders. Ugh! I tell you it's the truth, Rollison! He told me to come and finish you off, today." The man was sweating. "I wouldn't admit that if I was lying about anything else, would I?"

"I hope you wouldn't," said Rollison softly. "And I can find Matheson Bell at a house called *Faraway,* on Wimbledon Common."

"Yes, that's right."

"Who else will I find at *Faraway?*"

"He lives there with his wife and daughter, and they've some guests. I don't know who the guests are, but—but Estino was there for a night. I know that, He was—he was killed there."

"Was his daughter present when he was killed?"

The prisoner closed his eyes, as if to shut out some hideous vision.

"I—I think so. I wasn't there, I tell you! They called me in afterwards. But I knew Estino and his daughter were going to be guests for a few days. I – flew them over by private charter aircraft from Portugal on Monday."

"Well, well," said Rollison. "So you've a pilot's licence too."

"Yes! That's my job, I'm a pilot."

"What airfield did you land at?"

"A—a small one in Surrey."

"What customs officials can prove it?"

"They—they can't, Rollison. I had to get the Estinos in quietly. I don't know why, but it was really hush-hush."

When Rollison simply looked at him, he almost screamed: "I tell you I don't know why!"

"How did you come to take on a job like that?" asked Rollison.

"I flew Bell and his party on their last expedition," Cato muttered.

"Where was that to?"

"It was a little country between Laos and Thailand," the prisoner answered, still speaking very quickly. "I flew them in and went back and flew them out a month later. Something happened in between. They met Estino and his daughter out there for one thing. But I don't know what else happened. It isn't any use asking me to tell you, I can't tell you what I don't know."

"You're doing fairly well," Rollison said. "If you've kept your part of the bargain I'll keep mine. You'll stay here until I've checked. Don't try to get away, because my friends here don't like you as it is. They don't like anyone who injures Ebbutt. And remember you broke in here and began the violence. If you get hurt it will be no one's fault but yours. The police wouldn't worry about you for a split second."

"I—I know." The man moistened his lips again.

Rollison went out, locking the door on him. Ebbutt was waiting outside with a thumbs-up sign. Rollison went up through the hatch and out into the warm fresh air of the early evening. It was now a quarter to seven. He had a word with Ebbutt about keeping men on tap if he should need help, and went off to the accompaniment of a round of cheers from the thirty or forty boxers and athletes now bouncing about the gymnasium. Willie was skipping furiously.

When Rollison reached his car it was surrounded by a small group of youths, including the two lads whom he had seen earlier in the day. Apart from a few sticky fingermarks, the car was untouched. When he got inside it was stiflingly hot, so he opened the bonnet, let the inside of the car cool down and watched the eager youngsters peer into the engine; their "oo's" and "ah's" of approval echoed about the street.

A uniformed constable strolled towards Rollison and stopped.

"Shouldn't leave it there too much longer, sir – not after dark, anyhow."

"I'm just off."

"That's good sir. Lovely job, isn't it?"

Rollison drove back through streets which were no cooler but were almost deserted; driving through the City was like driving through an empty citadel. As he drove he pondered on how much, if anything, he should tell Grice of what had happened. Holding Cato and forcing him to answer the questions was illegal, strictly speaking, and it was better that Grice shouldn't know about it. The question was really whether Grice should be told that he was making any progress at all. He decided not to at this stage, and pulled up outside 23 Gresham Terrace. An old T-model Ford, brilliant in royal blue, was parked outside; that was Ebbutt's car. Some of his men had obviously come to keep Percy Wrightson company. Rollison hurried up the stairs, and as he reached the top landing saw the door open – just as it would if Jolly were present. Percy appeared.

"Back then, Mr. Rawlisson," he welcomed.

"Just made it, Percy."

"I beg to inform you that you 'ave—*have* a visitor waiting."

"Really?" said Rollison. "Who?"

"Perfessor Slimm, sir." Percy waited impatiently until Rollison entered the hall, then pushed open the door leading to the living-room, drew himself up and announced: "Mr. Rawlisson has returned, Perfessor."

Sammy Slimm was standing near the trophy wall and he held an American Bowie knife in his right hand; it was not unlike a ghurka kukri and was quite as deadly. As Rollison approached him he hung it by a leather loop to its peg and said: "I hoped you'd be early."

"I'm glad you're here," said Rollison. "What will you have to drink?"

"A bitter lemon," Sammy replied.

"Still T.T.?"

"Yes, sir."

"One bitter lemon, Percy, and a whisky and soda for me." Percy was so affected by the fact that the "Perfessor" was a teetotaller that he completely forgot to say "very good, sir." He poured the drinks and was going off when Rollison went on: "Can you find us a meal, or shall we go out, Percy?"

"A casserole of rump steak cooked in red wine is about to be served – sir."

"Thanks," said Rollison. "Ten minutes suit you?"

"Perfeckly," said Wrightson, and withdrew. Sammy, although looking very preoccupied, smiled as the door closed and remarked: "What's got into him? A Jolly complex?"

"He has ambitions in the field of domestic service," said Rollison drily. "A lot of people could do worse. Well, Sammy, is your essential work done?"

"No, blast it," said Sammy, sipping his bitter lemon. "But I've fixed with a London zoo to lend me a couple of chaps from the monkey-house to take over for the time being. I can't mess about at home sorting out the latest specimens. Marta's on my mind too much. I've phoned Lady Gloria. Marta hasn't woken up yet."

"Hasn't she?"

"No, but she's been examined and the doctor says she's all right. Rolly, I want to ask a favour of you."

"What is it?"

"Don't let the police question Marta."

"That's an impossible request and you know it."

"No it isn't. Grice is eating out of your hand, that's as plain as the nose on your face. If you say the word he'll ease off Marta. And it isn't as if she can help anyone. If she could have, she would have told me this afternoon." Sammy tossed his drink down as if it were a fiery stimulant. His eyes were flashing. "If she's asked a lot of questions God knows what effect it will have on her. You've seen what's happened already. She must have seen her father shot, or at the very least realised how he died, and it nearly turned her mind. If she isn't handled properly from now on it might have lasting harmful effect. Surely you realise that."

"If the doctors say she can be questioned without ill effect—" began Rollison.

"Oh, doctors! What do they know about the psychological effect on a highly sensitive young woman who isn't used to the kind of pressure we get in a highly organised society? You may not realise it, but Maria's a throwback to early village and tribal life. She only knows big cities and towns from brief visits, and she's always had her father to look after her. That's why she's so shocked – why it knocked her so hard. She's lost everything and everyone in a single damnable blow. She's got to be treated with extreme care, Rolly. *Physically* she'll be all right, I doubt if there is a stronger woman, but psychologically she's terribly vulnerable. Grice might not have the sensitivity to realise this, but surely you have."

"Sammy, I think you underrate the mental toughness of a girl like Marta Estino," Rollison said, reasonably. "She isn't going to lead a secluded sheltered life in future. Sooner or later she has to come into the great big world."

"*Why?*" Sammy exploded.

Rollison said slowly: "What's on your mind, Sammy?"

The other man was moving about the room, clasping his big hands together. His forehead was shiny with sweat, and there was a beading of sweat on his upper lip, too. His eyes still held the glittering, almost too beautiful expression; it was rather as if he had eyes which could see in the dark.

"I'm going to marry her," he announced brusquely.

"When?"

"As soon as she's herself again."

"So you're going to take her father's place?"

"Yes, I am – I can be father and husband and big brother in one. Rolly—" Sammy stood four square in front of Rollison and stretched out his hands, palms upwards, in appeal which it was impossible to ignore completely. "I'm desperately in love with her and I'm terrified for her. I know the kind of life she's led and what life she ought to lead. I can take her on an expedition every year, to a familiar country. I can make sure that when she's here in England she's surrounded by all the things she loves – the specimens of animals which we'll bring back with us. She's used to corresponding with the different zoos and biology centres throughout the world – she did most of the correspondence for her father. She can be damned useful to me *and* live her own life at the same time. It's essential Rolly. Don't fail her."

Rollison was tempted to ask if this was why Sammy had doped her; if this was why he had tried to make sure that Marta could not be questioned for a while. He did not. There was a sliver of doubt in his mind about Sammy's integrity, a question mark which nothing had yet removed. So he said: "The police must question her, Sammy, and you know it. And sooner or later she's got to realise that even if you do what you want, she might lose you and be faced with the same crisis over again. The way not to fail her is to help equip her for that kind of emergency."

"That's a bloody silly thing to say!"

"Sammy—"

"Well, isn't it?" stormed Sammy Slimm. He clenched his great hands, looking as if he would like to use them on Rollison. "It's just a lot of philosophical goo. I ought to have known better than to expect you to have any real compassion. You make me sick."

"So I make you sick," said Rollison, nettled. "I was going to make a suggestion which might help, but if you're going to fly off the deep end every time I disagree with you you might as well go and quarrel with someone else. You're right, I have a lot of influence with Grice, and if I tell him that it would be a mistake to work with you—"

"You wouldn't do that!"

"You provoke me anymore and see what I would do." Rollison forced himself to sound more angry than he felt, but underlying all he said there was a touch of genuine anger as well as of disquiet because he was not really sure about Sammy's motives.

Sammy growled: "What were you going to suggest?"

"That we ask the police to bring in a consultant psychologist to do their questioning for them. That would lessen a lot of the risk."

"Oh," said Sammy, blankly. "Oh, yes. Good idea. Best of both worlds, really. Er—will you do that?" When Rollison didn't answer at once, he went on almost desperately: "I know I blew my top too easily, but I'm terribly worried about Marta. Ever since I first saw her I've been – well, it's like feeling that you're holding something precious and fragile in your hands, and that the slightest thing might make you drop it and so lose it forever. There wasn't any hope of marrying her when her father was alive. No hope at all. But now – well, she needs someone desperately. I know she likes me, I believe I can make her fall in love with me. I feel as if I'm walking a tightrope, wanting to help her and protect her and at the same time being just out of reach. Can you see what I mean, Rolly?"

Rollison could see only too well what Sammy meant. He could see, too, that the desperation was not assumed, it was vivid and real. Whether it was simply anxiety for the girl or whether it was as much anxiety for himself, it was impossible to tell. One thing was certain. Grice would pick it up in a moment and so would anyone else whose mind was trained to notice the significant factors which could be used as evidence – especially circumstantial evidence.

If Sammy was as deeply in love with the girl as he said, if he longed to marry her, if he had known that he had no hope while her father was alive, then he had had a powerful emotional reason for wanting Estino dead.

Chapter Twelve

Faraway

"What are you going to do?" asked Sammy, forcing himself to be humble.

"Ask Grice to arrange for that consultant," answered Rollison. He moved to the telephone and saw Percy Wrightson hovering in the doorway which led to the domestic quarters. "Three minutes and you can serve dinner, Percy." Percy beamed and rushed off, while Rollison dialled Grice's home number; Grice himself answered.

He listened, said: "Yes," three times, and promised to make the arrangements at the Yard so that if the girl came round while he was off duty, everything should go according to plan. Rollison rang off.

"Thanks, Rolly," Sammy said in a subdued voice. "I won't forget that."

"Forget it!" said Rollison, grinning. "Are you going over to see Marta this evening?"

"I'd like to be around when she comes up. Have you made any progress in the investigation?"

"Not much."

"Any at all?"

Rollison said: "The man who can deal in snakes and tarantulas also has a nice line in scorpions."

"My God! They can be deadly."

"That's what I feared. Sammy, we need to know what other expeditions Estino and his daughter might have run across about the time that you ran across them. We aren't sure, but it begins to look as if something Estino discovered while he was in that jungle or the hill country explains his murder. Did you run across anyone else?"

Sammy said quietly: *"No."*

When Rollison didn't answer, Sammy went on: "That doesn't mean much, mind you. The place was teeming with United Nations people and Chinese and Yanks, as I've told you. I fought shy of meeting anyone. It was sheer chance that I ran into Estino and Marta, but I've already told you that."

"I see," said Rollison, wondering if that were true. Then he saw Percy Wrightson advancing proudly towards the table in the dining-alcove, a casserole dish held on a silver tray. He was within a yard of the table when he kicked against a carpet and lurched forward. Rollison held his breath. Sammy caught his. Wrightson looked for a moment as if he was going to hurl the casserole forward so as to free a hand with which to save himself. There was an instant of almost incredible suspense before he bent his knees and went down on them, placed the tray with near-reverent precision on the edge of the table, sent knives and forks clattering and knocked over an empty glass which did not break. He stayed where he was as if in an attitude of prayer.

"Percy," said Rollison, fervently, "Jolly couldn't have worked that miracle if you'd paid him a fortune."

Wrightson gulped. He looked round. He watched as Rollison lifted the tray and placed it near the middle of the table. He straightened up slowly and began to smile. At last he nodded vigorously and announced: "It's all a matter of balance, Mr. Ar. I'll give Jolly a lesson if yer like. 'Arf a mo' and I'll bring the veg."

Rollison dropped Sammy Slimm at the Marigold Club and drove off in the Bentley. There had been no alarm at the Club during the day. Two plain-clothes men on duty in Belsize Square acknowledged him. He went back towards Gresham Terrace and then to his garage near Berkeley Square, where he was known by the night as well as the day staff, and where he could get almost anything he wanted.

"A nice homely-looking job for a ride in the country," he said to the night foreman. "An elderly Austin or Rover. What can you do?"

"We've got a middle-vintage Rover, sir. How's that?"

"Sounds just right," said Rollison. "Fill her up will you? And forget to make a note in your records that I've taken it. If it's not back by the morning remember to put it in then. I'll pay in advance."

"Just as you like," the foreman said. He was a youthful man with curly hair and an easy smile. "Anything to do with snakes, Mr. Rollison?"

"You mustn't believe all you read in the newspapers," Rollison said. He drove off in a black Rover, rather like Grice's car, stopped when he was near Putney Bridge and telephoned the Blue Dog.

"Four chaps, in pairs, near the windmill on Wimbledon Common at ten o'clock sharp," echoed Ebbutt. "Okay, Mr. Ar. Expecting fun and games?"

"It wouldn't surprise me. How's Cato?"

"I gave him a big meal of fish and chips and a pint," replied Ebbutt. "He's sleeping it off. If you ask me he won't wake up until morning, either. That pint was pretty potent stuff." It was almost possible to see Ebbutt's gargantuan wink.

"Very nice work," approved Rollison. When he drove over Putney Bridge it was half past nine. The evening light was bright upon the calm surface of the river and soft upon the men and women and the boys and girl who were walking over the bridge or along the towing path, or were moving slowly in small boats. The banks held a promise for them when darkness came, but now the reflection of the sun was like gold upon a mirror.

Rollison made his way quite slowly up Putney Hill, then along by the side of the Common where the old houses remained here and there although small blocks of flats had replaced most of them. Some distance along, not far from the rough road which led to the windmill, was a house called *Faraway*. Cato had told him that it was on a corner and that the wooden fence was reinforced by a thick laurel hedge. There was a semi-circular drive and big gates at each entrance; the gates, painted some dark colour, were closed. Through the hedge and trees in the grounds, it was possible to see the lights at windows at the top of the house, but there was none on the ground floor. What looked like big garages showed at the back, the sloping roofs just visible above a hedge which did not appear to have been trimmed for years. Yet as he drove slowly past Rollison noticed that the drive itself was in good repair, and the gates had been newly painted; the name showed up in white on the dark-brown gates.

He drove away and parked some hundred yards from the gates, so that he could see if anyone went in or out. No one did. At five minutes to ten, a little red MG sports car which had seen better days, but which appeared to have a surprising performance, pulled up and headed for the windmill. In this were two of Ebbutt's men. A few minutes later from the other direction, a motor-cycle scorched along, with a pillion rider holding on tightly to a stocky man astride the machine. This was the other pair from Ebbutt. Rollison got out of his car in the dusk and walked towards the motor-cycle, which had stopped some distance from the men in the MG.

"Wotcher, Mr. Ar," said Micky Parks.

"Hallo, Micky," Rollison said. "I'm going to pay a visit to *Faraway*, the house on that corner over there." He pointed. "Will you and the others keep watch? Two of you follow anyone who leaves in a hurry, and the others wait in case I need help."

"Suits us," said Micky. "Expecting any rough stuff, Mr. Ar?"

"It wouldn't surprise me. Have you got those insecticide sprays?"

"One for each of us, yes." Micky beamed. *"And* one Indian club each *plus* a little piece of rubber tubing if we happen to want to put anyone to bye-byes for a little while. Expect snakes and things, Mr. Ar?"

"That wouldn't surprise me, either," Rollison said. "Micky."

"Yep?"

"No action unless there's an obvious emergency. Understand?"

"As if we would," protested Micky, virtuously.

Rollison grinned.

He drove back towards *Faraway*, keeping to the Common side of the road. Here several other cars were already parked and the couples in them had mysteriously disappeared, except for one pair who were sitting up and, it seemed, were arguing. No one took any notice of Rollison, and as he was parked off the roadway there was no need to leave his lights on. He did not lock the car for he might want to get away in a hurry. He stepped out from the trees and crossed to *Faraway*. Lights now showed at ground floor windows, and also at the main gate, where a lantern glowed. Rollison examined the gate and opened it; he did not think it was wired for an alarm. He drew on a pair of rubber gloves, bent down and pulled on a pair of rubber overshoes; they would make his feet hot, but at least he would be safe from bites. He walked across a grass patch, shoulders brushed by the hanging branches of trees. A porch light was on, too; there was no attempt at concealment. He went by the side of the house, past dark windows. There was just enough light in the sky to show the sheds, much bigger than ordinary suburban garages, and they had windows all along each side. He could make out two big wire cages, like soft fruit cages in country gardens, and thought he heard animals stirring, but there was no loud noise. The odour was unmistakably monkey, common to zoos and menageries and pet shops the world over.

Rollison went to the back of the house and tried the back door. It was locked. Above the door was a shallow porch, and it would be easy to climb up there. The moment he did, and forced entry, he would put himself on the wrong side of the law, but he did not let that worry him: what mattered was to do whatever was most likely to get results. That lovely girl at the Marigold Club was still in deadly danger. So was he.

He stretched up, gripped the edge of the porch and hauled himself up. The wood groaned, but held. Nimbly, he climbed until he was standing upright. At one side was a window, open a few inches at the top. He was able to reach across and open it wider without any trouble. He paused and listened but heard nothing, so he climbed through. He left the window wide open, in case he needed to make a run for it, then peered about a narrow passage. Three rooms led off this. The light from the afterglow was still enough to see by, and he tried the handles of the doors. None was locked.

The first room was filled with packing-cases and old trunks, with camping equipment and a great number of odds and ends which an expedition into any kind of remote country would need. On the tents and on most of the articles the name *M. Bell* was stamped. He used a torch to look at the labels on the old boxes and found two which had the Laotian customs mark and another with a Thai mark; all had arodia also. There was a musty smell in this room, but he found nothing alive.

The next room was full of cages on benches, and as he opened the door the stink of a reptile house assailed him. He switched on the room light and saw at least eight cages. It was startling, although half-expected. Snakes were coiled round stones, coiled up in corners on sand, looped round the branches of trees. Some adders were together in one cage, and he also recognised a puff-adder, a pair of cobras, some brilliantly-coloured snakes not unlike the adder in form; probably vipers from the East. He did not spend long there, just long enough to be sure what there was. There was enough venom in that room to kill dozens of people.

He stepped outside and wiped his forehead, then went into the next room, which seemed strangely still. It was difficult for him to give a name to the stillness, but he felt almost as if it was uncanny. He made sure there was no noise, and then closed the door and switched on the light.

The whole of two walls were made up into little cages with narrow metal bars in front of them; and in the first dozen cages he saw were spiders. On a small tag attached to each cage was a name, and he read two:

Argiopid – Male
Lycosa – Female

There was no odour here; nothing except that strange stillness, and the fact that he felt as if a thousand tiny eyes were watching him. He went out and closed the door. He made more noise than he had intended, and stood with his hand on the handle of the door for some seconds, listening. He fancied that he heard the sound of music, but it was a long way off. He felt sticky and very hot, and his feet were burning.

He reached the end of the passage and found a door locked on the other side, obviously to make sure none of the "pets" could get into the rest of the house. It would take some time to force the door.

He turned and went back the way he had come, climbed out and jumped down to the ground. It was difficult to get the overshoes off, his feet were so hot, but at last he had them clear. He folded them as best he could, went round to the front, put the shoes in a bush near the front door, stripped off the rubber gloves and hid them too, then gave himself a few minutes to relax. To help, he smoked half a cigarette. There were sounds in the street and from the Common, and cars passed to and fro, but no noise appeared to come from *Faraway*.

A clock not far off struck one; it was half past ten. He tossed his cigarette onto the gravel of the drive, trod it out and turned and pressed the bell which was at the side of the door.

As he stood waiting he reminded himself that he had only Cato's word that Estino and his daughter had been here; that was one of the first things that he must find out. He half regretted coming away from the house so soon. He might have been able to make some discovery if he had searched farther afield, but if he left it any later in the evening he could not expect to talk to Matheson Bell or to anyone else in this house.

He rang the bell again.

As he did so he heard a rustle of sound behind him. It reminded him vividly of the rustle at his flat which had led to those minutes of horror. He stood absolutely still for a moment, then slowly turned round.

Chapter Thirteen

Matheson Bell

As Rollison turned, and as the moment of horror faded, he realised that what he heard was the rustle of a newspaper. Out of the corner of his eye he saw the whiteness of paper. A moment later he saw the man standing holding it, a dark, shadowy figure in the dim fight. Only the paper and his face showed up clearly. He said: "Good evening."

"Good evening." Rollison wondered how long he had been out here and whether he had seen him hiding those overshoes and rubber gloves.

"Can I help you?"

"I would like to see Mr. Matheson Bell."

"I am Bell."

"Good evening, Mr. Bell."

"It's late for a call from a stranger," Bell remarked.

He had a deep and rather pleasant voice, and a curious naturalness; he gave the impression that he was trying to hold back laughter. The newspaper rustled more as he moved it, then folded it and tucked it under his arm. No one could hope to read in this light, except possibly headlines; why had he been carrying it as if about to read?

"Is it so late?" asked Rollison.

"For business, yes."

"Mr. Bell," Rollison said, "my name is Rollison. He paused, but Bell made no comment, so he went on: "I am here on behalf of a young lady whom you know."

"What young lady?"

"Miss Marta Estino."

Bell echoed: "Marta?" There was no surprise and no alarm in his voice, but he did not deny that he knew the girl. "Is she in England?"

"Didn't you know she was?"

"I did not"

If he was telling the truth Cato had lied; but Cato was in Cellar 3, a badly frightened man when he wasn't sleeping under the influence of Bill Ebbutt's drugged beer. This man was the more likely liar.

"May I come in and discuss it?" asked Rollison.

"It's better than discussing it out here," Bell admitted. He put his right hand to his pocket and Rollison grew tense, thinking for a moment that he might be getting a weapon; or an insect. Keys jingled. "Excuse me." Bell pushed past and fumbled with the key in the darkness, then pushed open the front door, stepped inside and held it open. "Come in."

As Rollison stepped across the threshold he felt very glad that Ebbutt's men were watching, so near at hand. Fear was an incalculable thing. He could step into conditions of deadly danger and feel no tremor at all, but here he felt thick, cloying fear; perhaps it was because of the eeriness of that silent room of tiny cages on the first floor.

The hall was large, with a few pieces of heavy mahogany furniture. A big chandelier with fine crystals hung scintillating from the high ceiling. A big staircase, also of mahogany and shiny red, was on one side, a wide passage on the other. Three tall shiny doors led off the passage. Bell, his back to Rollison, who had not yet seen his face clearly, moved to the middle of the doors, opened it and then turned round.

He was taller than Rollison; a big, massive man. He had a close-clipped moustache and a close-clipped beard, and had recently had a haircut also closely clipped. He was handsome in a bold way, with a broad nose and full lips, perhaps there was a hint of oriental blood in him. He wore a dark blue blazer and dark trousers, a khaki shirt with a scarf tied round the waist, sash-like.

"Come in," he said again.

Rollison murmured: "Thank you." As he stepped past he felt that fear again, a kind of menace; as if this man might strike him as he passed, or push him into the room, or slam and lock the door on him. He entered quite freely.

It was a library, with tall glass-fronted bookcases of the same rich red mahogany as the doors and the furniture outside. Every shelf was filled. A big leather-topped desk and big leather armchairs looked the acme of comfort. On the mantelpiece were some photographs, one of a woman and a much younger woman. His family? On one side were green metal filing cabinets, which struck an incongruous note. At right angles to the big desk was a smaller one with a typewriter and some paper on it. Rollison took in all this at a glance, then saw another case in a corner, also glass-fronted. In it were three rifles, all of the kind used for big-game hunting, and on shelves which filled one side of the case were cameras of various kinds, while there were two tripods and some other photographic equipment in a corner.

"Forgive me if I didn't give you a very warm welcome," Bell said. "My wife and daughter thought they saw a man prowling in the grounds half an hour ago, and I checked when I went for an evening paper."

"Was there anyone?"

"You're the only prowler I saw," observed Bell, with a quick smile. He might mean that he knew very well that Rollison had been up to the back of the house; or he might simply be saying that he wanted to put Rollison at a disadvantage. "Will you have a drink?"

"If you're going to join me."

"Whisky and soda?"

"Please."

Bell had strong hands. They were not out of proportion to the rest of him, as Sammy Slimm's were, but powerful-looking, tanned, with fine hazel-shaped nails. His fingers were quite steady as he poured out of a bottle and splashed in soda water from a syphon. He handed Rollison a drink.

"Cheers."

"Cheers." Bell sipped. "What is this about Marta Estino?"

"She's had rather a bad shock," Rollison said, quietly. "I am trying to help her recover from it and to make sure that she doesn't have another."

"What kind of shock?"

If Bell really knew all about it, if Cato had told the truth, then this was quite remarkable acting. His voice was casual, his manner exactly what one might expect from a man who had to show a polite interest, but was not deeply concerned.

Rollison said: "She was deeply attached to her father."

"So I understand."

"Did you know them well?"

"We knew each other, yes, but I wouldn't say we were more than acquaintances. We met at international conferences of our kind, you know, and now and again we met on expeditions, usually when we were preparing to start off into different parts of the hinterland. But I wouldn't say that I knew him or his daughter well. Mr. Rollison, I haven't too much time to spare. I'll be glad if you'll come to the point."

"Gladly," Rollison said. "Why didn't you report to the police?"

"I *beg* your pardon?" Bell looked and sounded genuinely shocked.

"Why didn't you tell the police that you knew the man found murdered on Hampstead Heath."

Bell frowned, drank more deeply, put his glass down and turned to the mantelpiece. He took down a tobacco jar and a pipe, turned again and began to fill the pipe. Every movement was deliberate and considered.

"I wish you wouldn't talk in riddles, Mr. Rollison. Are you suggesting that a man found murdered on Hampstead Heath was Professor Estino, and that I should know about it?"

"Yes."

"I don't know whether you've come here simply to be offensive," said Bell, "but you're talking nonsense. How on earth should I be expected to know that Estino—" He broke off, as if the significance of what he had heard was dawning on him; it was a beautiful piece of timing. *"*Estino *murdered."*

"Yes."

"Good God!"

"And his daughter saw it happen."

"Good God!" repeated Bell. He tossed the rest of the drink down. "What a shocking business. Marta saw her father—" He broke off, picked up the pipe as if he wanted something to do with his hands, and went on: "Where is she?"

"In a kind of nursing home."

"Poor kid," Bell said. "She was devoted to her father. Absolutely devoted. That much I did know about her. What a hideous thing, to see him murdered."

"Yes, wasn't it."

Bell said: "Mr. Rollison, I've realised who you are now. You're what could loosely be called a private detective, aren't you? So presumably you're here to try to get information which might help you find the murderer. Is that right?"

"Yes."

"Surely the police—"

"There are times when I can do what the police can't," Rollison interrupted. "I can prowl, for instance."

"Ah. So my wife did see you."

"Possibly. Mr. Bell, haven't you or your family seen any newspapers in the past two days?"

"No"

"None at *all*?" Rollison's voice rose in disbelief.

"If you are being pedantic we have seen newspapers on news-stands in Paris and also here, but we have not read a newspaper. We flew back from Paris only this afternoon – late this afternoon – and had plenty to occupy us on the way. We did not worry about newspapers. I am preparing for an expedition into South America and my wife and daughter are helping me to get ready. We went to make some purchases in Paris and also arrange a contract with an

American television agent for the television rights of whatever pictures we manage to take. We have been in Paris for three days."

It was all Rollison could do to stop himself from saying: "I don't believe it."

Bell seemed to be waiting for some such reaction.

Rollison said: "I see, Mr. Bell. Was this house empty while you were away?"

"It was not. But I hardly see that it is any business of yours."

Rollison said: "It could be the business of the police." Bell put his pipe to his lips, struck a match, seemed to give all his attention to lighting the tobacco, but when it was finished and a great cloud of pale blue-grey smoke was billowing and giving off a rich aroma, he said from the side of his mouth: "I don't know whether you think that you can alarm me or frighten me in any way, but I do assure you that you can't. You can exasperate me, though, and even anger me. Please say what you want to say, and then go."

Rollison didn't speak.

"Mr. Rollison, either you will—"

"Estino was shot in this house," Rollison said flatly.

Bell, one hand half raised to make his point, the other at his pipe, seemed to freeze.

"In this house," repeated Rollison. "He came here with his daughter. They were flown in by a man who flew them in a private aircraft from Lisbon three days ago. The pilot brought them here. The police don't yet know it, but they'll learn tonight – I have arranged for them to be told." The fact that he had arranged nothing of the kind was unimportant; what mattered was to convince this man that he could do nothing to prevent the police from being told what had happened. "He was shot here in cold blood, taken from here in a car and left on Hampstead Heath. Somewhere between here and the Heath his daughter escaped. Since she was taken into the charge of the police at least one attempt has been made to murder her, presumably to make sure that she couldn't tell the police where she had been or who killed her father." Rollison paused, but Bell looked too shocked to comment, and stood with his pipe stem pointing towards Rollison and his lips parted. "Do you think this is a reasonable explanation of my visit, Mr. Bell?"

Bell swallowed hard.

"If this is true, of course it is – but it can't be true!" He gave a short, harsh laugh. "It's a preposterous thing to say. Quite preposterous. Our servants—" He broke off. "Rollison, I don't believe any of this rigmarole. I doubt if I would believe it even if the police were to confirm what you've said. It's so utterly absurd."

"Have you read that newspaper you had in the garden?" asked Rollison.

"You haven't given me a chance to. A boy delivers it every evening and pushes it between the bars of the gate. I strolled out to get it and to look for prowlers." Bell picked the newspaper up from his desk and opened it. After a moment his eyes seemed to harden and his lips tightened. This was the *Evening News* which carried the story of the shooting attack on Estino, a re-hash of the finding of the body, everything that could be wanted to confirm the basic truth of what Rollison had said. He lowered the newspaper.

He said: "I reject as unthinkable your suggestion that murder was carried out in my house. Quite unthinkable. I would like to talk to the police immediately. I would also like the house searched and everything done that the police think necessary to make quite sure that the story is exposed as a ridiculous invention."

He looked round at a telephone.

"But you left someone at the house when you were in Paris," Rollison reminded him.

"There is always my man and his wife, who look after the house, the animals and the specimens when we are away," agreed Bell. "They had guests – they are always at liberty to have guests when we are away."

"Why don't you send for them before you send for the police?" demanded Rollison.

"They are no longer here. They have gone on a short holiday – a holiday which they're fully entitled to, although we didn't expect them to go quite so quickly. They—" Bell broke off, frowning, and giving the impression that he was beginning to wonder whether there could be any truth in what Rollison had said. Then he went on explosively: "Oh, it's quite ridiculous! Is there any particular policeman in charge of this investigation, Mr. Rollison?"

"Yes. Superintendent Grice of Scotland Yard."

"Then I must talk to him," said Bell brusquely. He did not turn to the telephone, but paused again before asking flatly: "Where did you get this information from? Marta?"

"No," said Rollison. "But Marta was shot at, and the obvious implication is that someone wanted to make quite sure that she couldn't tell the police what had happened and where it happened." When Bell made no comment, but seemed to be trying to absorb the unpleasant news, he went on: "Can you prove that you and your family were all in Paris, Mr. Bell? If you can, that should help a lot."

Instead of saying: "Of course I can," Bell kept silent. It was like a confession of guilt. The silence lengthened, until it was broken by footsteps outside in the passage, then by the opening of the door.

Chapter Fourteen

Mother And Daughter

The woman who came in was on the young side of middle-age. She was sturdy looking, rather mannish, but much better looking than Maggie Lister. She had fine brown eyes, doe-like in their softness. Her iron-grey hair was cut quite short, but attractively wavy. She had on just enough make-up to prevent her from seeming dowdy, and wore a beigy-brown linen two-piece, the jumper high at the neck. She had a broad bosom, but not particularly big, a broad face, a broad brow.

She looked at Rollison and spoke to Bell.

"Mat, I thought you would like to know that the late news will be on in five minutes." Before her husband could respond, and still looking at Rollison, she asked: "Did you find anyone?"

"Only this gentleman," said Bell, heavily. "Charlotte, we have the honour of a visit from the renowned Mr. Richard Rollison. I believe that you and Nora often amuse yourselves by reading stores which are written about him."

The woman said: *"The Toff?"* The soubriquet came out so naturally that even Rollison was flattered. Her eyes lit up. She came forward with her hands held in front of her, welcoming, showing no sign at all of alarm. When Rollison put his hand forward she took it eagerly. Hers was strong, firm, cool. "I can't imagine what's brought you," she said, "but it's a pleasure indeed to meet you. And Nora will be thrilled."

"That's very charming of you," Rollison said. It was also very disarming. He wondered if it were possible that the woman could have heard any of the conversation from a nearby room or from the passage, whether her coming had been really for the purpose she had declared. There seemed to be no doubt of the genuineness of her feeling, however. She held his hand just a fraction of a minute too long then let it go and backed away.

"But prowling *here* – good gracious!"

"I wondered when you would get round to the significance of that," said Bell drily.

"You can't be serious." She almost accused Rollison.

"Oh, but he is very serious," said Bell. "And it's beginning to look as if he has some reason to be. I'll tell you about it soon, dear, but first we have a difficult job on hand."

Mrs. Bell looked mystified. She also looked charming – wholesome was the word which sprang to Rollison's mind – and it was more difficult than ever for him to associate these two with murder and violence, with organising that campaign of terror. They were "nice" people.

"What job?" Mrs. Bell asked.

"Convincing Mr. Rollison that although I *cannot* easily prove that I've been in Paris for the last three days, I have been."

"Of course you have!"

"Oh, *we* know," said Bell. "But—" He turned to Rollison, and gave another short, rather over-hearty laugh. "The difficulty is a real one, Mr. Rollison. I told you that I have been negotiating with an American television agent for certain rights in documentary travel pictures we plan to take on our next expedition. It was a secret visit, because there is another expedition planned for the same part of South America – Peru and Brazil – and I wanted to get in first. I think I succeeded. The agent is a man named Bryer, an American resident in Paris, and he doesn't represent any particular company. I don't even know whom he hopes to deal with." Bell was frowning. "I know all this may sound peculiar, but he's brought off some good deals for me in the past, and believes that he can bring this one off very profitably." Bell shrugged, and forced a smile. He gave the impression that he was very much on edge as he went on: "Bryer has flown to New York on this and various other television projects. He may go as far as Hollywood to sell the idea. It certainly isn't possible to get in touch with him quickly."

Bell gave that nervous bark of a laugh again.

"Is it all that important?" asked Charlotte Bell.

"Mr. Rollison seems to think so."

The woman turned to Rollison, her laugh almost as nervous as her husband's. It was as if she felt completely out of her depth – as if in fact she knew only what she had heard since she had entered this room.

"I do wish you would explain what this is all about."

Before Rollison attempted to answer, and as Bell rammed the tobacco down in his pipe as if he didn't care whether he ever got it alight, someone else walked along the passage. Rollison saw a girl appear by the open door. She was rather like her mother, but a head shorter, and her features as well as her complexion were more delicate. Her broad face and rather spade-shaped chin detracted from her good looks, but she had her mother's wide-set, beautiful brown eyes. She wore a sleeveless brown dress which fell just to her knees. On some girls it would have looked like a sack, but on her it fitted nicely and well.

The moment she caught sight of Rollison, she exclaimed: "Good heavens – The *Toff!*"

In spite of himself Rollison laughed. So did Bell – his began as a rueful chuckle and developed into a deep rollicking laughter. Mrs. Bell laughed, too. Without any sign of embarrassment the girl, who was in her late teens or her early twenties, came forward with her hand outstretched.

"I've just been hearing about you on the news," she said. "I suppose that's why you're here. Daddy, an awful thing has happened. It really upset me, and I think it will you and Mother. Professor Estino has been murdered. And there's some mystery about his daughter, too. Isn't it shocking?"

Charlotte Bell exclaimed: "Murdered? Oh, no."

"Mr. Rollison has made it quite clear that it's 'oh, yes,'" said Bell.

"The news did say that the police had consulted you, Mr. Rollison, and also Sammy Slimm," went on Nora in the most natural way imaginable. "And they said that *your* flat had been invaded by snakes and spiders."

Her mother said: "Oh, surely not," in a weak voice.

"Invasion is one word," Rollison said. "I admit that I didn't like it much when one popped out of the tap when I was having a bath."

"That old trick," said Bell, almost off-handedly.

"Old trick?" asked Rollison sharply.

"Children in parts of Mexico where the spiders are common push 'em into taps and other unexpected places, for the fun of seeing their elders jump," said Bell. "Children are much less scared of them than adults, they don't always realise the danger. Not that there's much if you know how to handle them and don't upset them. Only angry snakes and spiders attack – did you know that, Mr. Rollison?"

"Angry *or* frightened?" said Rollison.

"I don't think there's much difference where snakes are concerned," replied Bell. "Fright makes them angry." He ran his hand over his close-cropped hair. "Darling, I think you'd better make some coffee, and then Mr. Rollison can tell us all exactly what he's told me. It will give me a little time to think, too. Unless you think we should inform the police at once, Mr. Rollison."

"I don't think we need worry about that for an hour or two."

"I wish I knew what all this mystery was about," said Nora. She looked at the Toff in a half-admiring, half-fearful way.

"We soon shall," said her mother, practically.

The coffee was very good. So were some biscuits which the Bell women made at home, it seemed – a kind of Scottish butter biscuit which melted in the mouth.

They listened to the story with rapt attention. Now and again when their house was mentioned and when Rollison made it clear that someone had said that the murder had been committed in this very place, Nora started to protest, but her mother always contrived to stop her from saying more than a word or two, and yet did not actually rebuke her. As he looked at them, as he talked, as he studied

Matheson Bell, Rollison found it more than ever difficult to believe that this was a family of murderers. On the other hand the fact that Bell had difficulty in proving that he hadn't been here put a question mark even larger than the one against Sammy Slimm. At last it was over.

Nora was the first to speak. "I simply can't believe that it happened," she declared. "Mr. Rollison, who told you that Professor Estino was murdered here? In all fairness you must tell us the name of your informant."

"Later, I think," said Rollison. "The first thing is to make sure whether he's actually been here. Can you get in touch with your staff?"

Bell said flatly: "No."

"Do you know where they've gone?"

"They're a Spanish couple," said Bell, uneasily. "They may have flown home for a few days, they may be anywhere in Europe or they may still be in this country. I simply don't know. They made their own arrangements while we were in Paris. The police may be able to trace them, but I can't even be sure of that. It's certainly time the police came and searched here, isn't it?"

"Surely there's no need—" Nora began. Then she stopped as if realising that there was indeed a great need. She looked at Rollison almost warily, and he could imagine that she was beginning to feel that her idol was showing feet of clay. "It's a beastly situation, Daddy. Certainly we've got to clear it up as soon as possible."

"Yes." Bell looked at his wife. "What do you say, Charlotte?"

His wife was sitting back in an easy chair and frowning. She did not answer immediately, but drew her legs in and sat upright, moving very slowly. She was much more worried than she had been when she had first entered, and Rollison wondered again whether she knew that her husband was lying, and whether all of these people were conspiring to deceive him.

"Charlotte," repeated Bell, almost sharply.

"I think I'm frightened," Charlotte Bell said deliberately, looking at her husband. "You remember that I cleared out the spare room myself, because the Lopezes had gone off in such a hurry that they hadn't done anything up there."

"Yes."

"I think I saw some Portuguese tramway tickets in the ashtray," said Charlotte Bell, very slowly. "And I'm sure there was an empty packet of cigarettes of a Portuguese brand. I didn't really think much about it, but now I come to think it does suggest that someone was here from Portugal, doesn't it?"

Bell stared at her, took his pipe from his lips, then got up, nearly knocking over a coffee cup, and stepped to the desk. He picked up the telephone and began to dial. As he did so he formed letters and numerals with his lips: "w-h-i-1-2-1-2." He held the receiver to his ear and asked Rollison: "Superintendent whom did you say?"

"Grice," said Rollison.

Grice wasn't at the Yard, but the night duty superintendent in charge promised to telephone him, and the local police sent a squad of men at once. Bell let them in. The women were very subdued, Nora particularly so: she gave the impression that she blamed Rollison for what was happening here. Yet something else preoccupied her, Rollison believed, and her mother, too. Charlotte Bell did not seem to resent what Rollison had done, but kept looking at her husband as if wondering what was really going on in his mind. Bell moved about in a rather vague way, pipe in mouth or in hand, being as helpful as possible. Fingerprint experts and photographers concentrated on the spare room, and two men whom Rollison knew well were searching the room for any other clues. Grice himself arrived, alone, just after half past eleven. By that time contact photographs had been taken and printed of fingerprints found in the room. Comparisons were made, under microscopes between these and those of Marta and Professor Estino.

"Estino was here all right," Grice said to Rollison, before very long. "So was his daughter." He glanced towards the Bells, who were outside in the passage, Nora looking woebegone and rather scared, her mother tight lipped, Bell quite himself. "The Portuguese cigarette packet seems quite new. It won't take long to check when the tickets were used, a telephone call to Lisbon in the morning will establish that. Now we have to find out how the Estinos left here."

"Excuse me, sir." It was one of the elderly Yard men, who was straightening up from the floor where he had been on his knees. "There are some stains here which I think are bloodstains. And that looks like a bullet hole."

He was pointing matter-of-factly at a small hole drilled in the solid wood of a wardrobe. It looked the size of a .22 bullet.

Chapter Fifteen

Suspects

"All right, Rolly," Grice said. "Now you can tell me where you got this information from? You didn't just wave a wand and say *abracadabra*."

They were walking along the road by the Common, towards Grice's car. It was after one o'clock and most of the couriers' cars had gone, but here and there one was still parked; Rollison's hired one was, too. Not far off, Ebbutt's men, tired from their waiting and doubtless wearied with disappointment, were still on duty. Rollison wished that he could find a way of telling them to go home without letting Grice know they had been here. The stars were out and the night was beautifully clear. A slight wind blew. The temperature was hovering about the middle sixties, warm for London especially out here on the Common.

Lights were still on at *Faraway*. Police were still in that spare room, Rollison knew, and others were on duty outside. The Bells had said very little after the discovery of the bullet hole, but Nora had still seemed to regard Rollison reproachfully. It was surprising how much that mattered to him.

"No, I didn't wave a wand," Rollison replied to Grice. "I waved a threat of *Vipera* – viper to you – and it worked. I'm not going to tell you who it was yet, Bill. If I do you'll have to charge him and if you make a charge I won't be able to get any more information out of him. As it is, I might be able to."

"You're asking me to compound a felony," Grice grumbled.

"Come off it! You don't yet know what felony you think you might have compounded. Leave me my freedom of action. It looks as if Estino was killed in that room, doesn't it? "

"We need to check the blood group of the blood which soaked into the carpet and the floor-boards, and also need to check the rifling on the bullet we prised out of the wardrobe," Grice said. "Once we have fixed that we'll know for certain. It looks the same rifling to me, but I wouldn't like to trust my memory. I can check as soon as I'm back at the Yard. Coming?"

"I'd rather get some sleep, and learn in the morning," Rollison said.

"Please yourself. What else do you know against the Bell family?"

"I know nothing against them at all. I like 'em. But that doesn't mean that Bell isn't lying."

"Odd that he can't give us anything at all to prove he was in Paris in all those three days," said Grice. "His wife and daughter can prove *they* were, but he wasn't with them. They were on a shopping spree." Grice didn't smile. "The odd thing is they don't seem as if they're lying for him. If they'd said *they* knew where he was and had been with him all the time, it might be difficult for us to disprove. But they admit that they don't know – or at least can't swear – where he was. They all went to Paris, he dodged off to this agent who cannot now be traced, and met up with his family three nights later. He could have been to and fro to London twice a day for all they know." Grice reached his car. "Can I give you a lift?"

"No, thanks."

Grice said: "Did Ebbutt's men bring you?"

Rollison chuckled. "No. Mind if I tell them they can go off now?" He started off, seeing Micky Parks under a street lamp on the Common side of the road. Grice had known all the time that they were there of course, and that wasn't surprising. Very little escaped Grice if it came anywhere near him. He drew near enough to call: "Micky, you can go home if you want to. I'm through here."

"You sure?"

The police will look after me from now on."

"They couldn't look after pussy," said Parks in a clear and carrying voice. "Okay, Mr. Ar. Thanks for the opportunity, anyhow." He went off and Rollison turned back to Grice, who was at the wheel of his car. Rollison climbed in, but kept a door open.

"The fact that the Spanish servants have gone off at such short notice is damned queer, too," Grice said, as if their conversation had not been interrupted. "It should be possible to trace them and it should be possible to trace the television agent, but both will take some time. Odd thing that Bell should use an American agent in Europe, isn't it?"

"I shouldn't think so," Rollison said, thoughtfully. "Lookout men and contact men for Hollywood litter most European cities. I'll telephone you in the morning, Bill."

"You tell me the name of your informant and I'll tell you all I can in the morning," Grice said shrewdly.

"We'll see! Any news from Marta Estino?"

"She came round this evening," Grice replied. He did not use the words "woke up," but that might not be significant. "She will be questioned tomorrow by a psychologist, as we promised. She isn't going to be worried tonight by anyone. Her evidence is less urgent now although it might still be of vital importance. If she actually saw the shooting, and Bell was the man, then we've got Bell. If she saw another man then Bell won't be off the hook, but he'll be in a less vulnerable position. If she didn't see the killer—" Grice broke off.

"Yes indeed," said Rollison.

"Why be so cryptic?"

"If she didn't see the killer, why did the killer try to kill her?" asked Rollison. He gave a short laugh. "I'm getting too tired, that's too near a tongue twister for me at this time of night. Good night, Bill."

"Rolly."

"Yes."

"Hiding a material witness is still a serious offence, you know. I realise that you're doing everything you can with the best of motives, but you could be sticking your neck out dangerously far."

"I'll draw it back if I see anything sniping at me," Rollison assured him. "After all, I know you wouldn't do any such thing."

He got out of the car and walked along to his own. He felt quite certain that nothing had been put in it, for Ebbutt's men, watching, would have warned him. Nevertheless he switched on the courtesy light, then shone his torch under the seats, because his memory of the snakes and the spiders was so vivid. He thought of the collection of both only a hundred yards away from here, so well guarded and well labelled, and also thought of the pleasant-seeming family who lived with them. In a way, that seemed to take something out of the horror which snakes and spiders could create in the mind. He could almost picture Mexican children playing with them.

He drove off, slowly. He felt tired but not tensed up, for it seemed that for a while at least acute danger was past. After a few minutes he warned himself that such a thought might lull him into a sense of security which wasn't justified. He mustn't take the slightest chance and mustn't expose himself to any known danger unless it was wholly worthwhile. He found himself thinking a lot about the Bells, and comparing in his mind the fact that Sammy Slimm and Matheson Bell both claimed that they hadn't looked at newspapers. He began to frown. Bell had talked about them being too busy to worry about newspapers, but was that reasonable? If they had flown on one of the regular flights from Paris then newspapers – English and French – would have been distributed free of charge. One of the three would surely have looked at the front page of an English newspaper if they hadn't seen one for three days. The natural reaction of any English person – of anyone no matter what nationality – who had been cut off for a few days from home news, would be to glance through a paper.

Grice hadn't told him whether Bell had explained how he had flown back, but supposing he had come by private aircraft to a small airfield, like the Estinos, then his story would be much more understandable.

Rollison turned into Berkeley Square. He yawned as he turned in the Rover to a small, wizened man now on duty, and walked back to Gresham Terrace yawning all the way. He kept a close look-out, however, and was sure that no one followed him. He turned the corner of his street, looked up and saw that the light was on in his living-room, a brighter light than Jolly would have left on. Percy Wrightson might be making free of the room, and might even have some cronies there. Rollison frowned. That wasn't really likely, for it was very late. Percy would probably be in bed.

A man stepped out of the doorway next to 22, a big, slow-moving man.

Rollison's heart jumped.

"Mr. Rollison?"

"Yes."

"Mr. Grice would like you to telephone him at his office the minute you get in. Will you do that, sir, please."

"Yes."

"Thank you, sir."

Rollison went up. It was less than three quarters of an hour since he had seen Grice and this must surely mean some urgent or startling development. He walked up the stairs. The lights were on at every landing, that was a Jolly-type precaution to make sure that no one could conceal themselves here by night. Rollison reached his own landing. The door opened almost at once and Percy Wrightson, wearing a pair of pale blue pyjamas under a tweed jacket, cupped his hand over his mouth to smother a yawn, and said:

"Bit late, aincha?"

"Sorry, Percy."

"Oh, it ain't me," said Percy. "A job's a job, and no one ever told me that Jolly cared what time *he* went to bed. It's the Perfessor, Mr. Ar. He's in a real tizzy, he is. I can't do nothing with him. As a matter of fact," added Percy, lowering his voice, "if I didn't know he was T.T., I'd say he was drunk. You should have been here when he arrived. Knocked your block off, he would have."

Percy's report fanned to flame the spurt of annoyance which Rollison already felt for Sammy Slimm, but this was no time to show it. Rollison had hoped to come back to a few hours sleep and a chance to reflect so that in the morning when talking to Grice he could be sure of how much he wanted to say. Now there was another crisis to overcome and he was in no mood for it. As he went across the hall, the door of the living-room opened violently, and Sammy came striding out. He glared at Percy.

"I thought I told you to tell me when he got back!"

Wrightson was a patient man, and tolerant too, but he resented injustice. Moreover, he had a temper which could flare up on the instant. Now it threatened to flare. Rollison would not have been surprised had he jumped forward and punched Sammy on the nose. For a moment it looked as if he would do just that. Then he drew a deep breath, bunched his hands and held them at his sides and said in a tone which would not have disgraced Jolly: "Mr. Rawlisson has returned home, Perfessor."

Sammy switched his glower to Rollison. "And about time, too. Where the hell have you been?"

Rollison caught his breath.

Wrightson did a half about turn.

Rollison said: "Percy."

"Sir."

"Don't you hold out on me!" Sammy roared.

"Show Mr. Slimm the door," said Rollison. "Tell him that I will be home at nine o'clock in the morning and will be prepared to see him then, by appointment."

Four things happened almost at the same moment. Sammy's eyes seemed to flame with anger, Wrightson's glowed with the light of an answered prayer, Sammy thrust out a hand to grab Rollison's arm and Percy Wrightson intervened with as neat a little left arm jab to the stomach as Rollison had seen for a long time. Sammy gasped and doubled up.

"This way, Perfessor," said Wrightson. He took Sammy's left wrist, hauled him upright and hustled him towards the open front door. At the same time he turned an enquiring eye on Rollison, who winked. He went into the living-room and looked at the telephone, but did not think he would be able to ring Grice before an interruption came; much would depend on whether Sammy had learned his lesson.

There were sundry sounds at the door before a tap came, and Wrightson appeared, his face aglow with satisfaction.

"Excuse me, sir."

"Yes, Percy?"

'Perfessor Slimm would be very much obliged if you would be good enough to spare him a few minutes now, sir, and not wait until the morning."

Oh?' said Rollison. "Well, perhaps you'd better show him in."

Percy clasped his hands above his head, shook them vigorously and went out smartly. Rollison sat on the corner of his desk, remembering how he had felt the previous night in this room. There was a newspaper over the seat of his armchair, now; it *could* conceal one of those damned adders. The simple truth was that the affair of the snakes and spiders had unnerved him; he had to watch his own reactions or he could behave as badly as Sammy.

"Perfessor Slimm, sir," Percy announced, suddenly.

Sammy came in, all legs and arms. He might be chastened, but he was not really subdued; in fact his lips were quivering and his eyes held a glint that was not far removed from venomous. Sammy had always been hot-tempered, his behaviour now was much more than a fit of anger. It was all-consuming fury, and Rollison wondered uneasily what had caused it.

"I want to know what you've been saying to Grice," Sammy said in a high-pitched, reedy voice.

"You already know," replied Rollison.

"No I don't. You've done some swinish things behind my back. I mean to know what it is. I mean to know what you think you're playing at. Grice's men refused to let me see Marta." Sammy's voice rose almost to a pitch of hysteria. "They wouldn't let me in. I went round there and begged and pleaded. Your aunt tried, Miss Lister tried, everyone begged them to let me see her, but the police were adamant. Grice wouldn't have done that if you hadn't put him up to it. What are you trying to do to me, Rollison. Drive me mad?"

Chapter Sixteen

Blood Group

As Rollison looked at Sammy Slimm and that last question echoed about the room, he realised that is was not rhetorical. Sammy was at a terrible stretch of nervous tension. It showed in his eyes, in the way he clenched his hands, in the stridence of his voice. It should have been quite obvious when Rollison had arrived and seen the condition he was in. Sammy was sick: he *was* being driven almost beyond endurance by all that was going on.

One thing stuck out like a sore thumb; this wear on his nerves must have started some time ago. Sammy knew more than he had yet said, his state of nerves could not have come about in a few short hours.

"Why the hell don't you answer me?" he demanded shrilly. "Get on that telephone. Tell the police I've got to see that girl!"

"Sammy," Rollison said, mildly, "you've got one thing wrong. I do not control the police and I haven't as much influence with then as you think. They may sometimes be advised by me and occasionally guided by me, but I can't do their job for them. If they think they should take a certain course of action they'll take it whether I like it or not."

After a pause, Sammy said incredulously: "But I always thought they ate out of your hand!"

"Now you know they don't. I can't make them let you see Marta." He sat on the arm of a chair. "Why don't you sit down?"

"I can't sit *still*. Do you mean to say there's nothing you can do?"

"I might be able to help if I knew why they won't let you see her."

"How the devil do I know what goes on in their infantile minds?"

"Sammy," said Rollison softly, "if you talk to the police like that you'll make them so hostile that they'll never give you an inch. Why won't they let you see her?"

"I don't know."

"Haven't they given you any reason at all?"

"Not a damned word."

"Don't you know what made them change their minds? They didn't worry if you saw her earlier."

"If I knew, I'd tell you," Sammy said. He turned away and Rollison saw that his body was quivering and thought he was screwing up his face, as if to fight back tears. "I just want to see her, that's all. I just want to see her. She means so much to me. I'm terrified in case they hurt her."

"Why should you think they'd hurt her?"

Sammy stared at a little gem of the Constable school painting on the wall.

"I told you, earlier. She's a sensitive, highly strung, vulnerable person. She isn't like ordinary people."

"You know what I think about that and you also know that the police are going to make sure she's questioned by someone who will know how to deal with her. Sammy—"

"You really are on their side, aren't you?" Sammy said bitterly. He swung round. "I thought I could rely on you as a friend."

"I hope you can," said Rollison quietly. "But if I'm to help at all I've got to know everything – motives, hopes, fears, the lot. Grice obviously has got reason to suspect that you might influence what Marta Estino has to say and he's making sure that you can't."

"What the devil do I mean?"

"What I say," said Rollison. He stood up. "Why did you drug Marta?"

"*What?*" cried Sammy, in a voice so shrill that it almost hurt Rollison's ears.

"I saw the hypodermic needle puncture in her back," Rollison told him levelly. "It wasn't very difficult to find out, Sammy. She went off to sleep – as you called it – much too quickly, and she stayed asleep far too long for it to be natural. I expect the police realise what you did by now, and that would influence them. It would make them sure that you don't want Marta to talk. You don't, do you?"

"I don't want her driven out of her mind," Sammy muttered. He attempted no denial, and did not even offer any real excuse. He behaved as if what he did had been fully justified.

"Oh, don't be such a bloody fool," said Rollison, as if suddenly losing patience. At the back of his mind there was the urgent need for some kind of shock treatment on this distraught man. "Drive you mad, drive her mad – what do you think the human mind is made of? It's tougher than you realise. It takes a long time to turn a man's mind. Even yours. What's *on* yours, Sammy? What are you hiding?"

"I'm not hiding a thing!"

"You're a liar," Rollison said.

Two things happened at once. The telephone started to ring and Sammy Slimm launched himself at Rollison. The distraction of the bell made Rollison a split second late in flinging his arms up to defend himself. Sammy's clenched right fist smashed into his face. He went staggering back, knocked against a chair and toppled backwards. The bell rang on and on. Sammy came at Rollison as he struggled to get up, punched him on the shoulder, punched him on the neck. *Brrr-brrr. Brrr-brrr.* Sammy's eyes were glaring and his mouth was open, he looked as if he really had gone mad. He struck out again, but this time Rollison was ready. Rollison clutched his bony wrist, and twisted. Sammy went flying across the room, fetched up against the wall with a heavy thud, banged his head and began to stagger about as if he were going to fall. *Brrr-brrr. Brrr-brrr.* Rollison struggled to his feet. His knuckles were sore where he had banged the fender, his jaw ached, his right eye was painful. Sammy was slumped against the wall, eyes closed, gasping for breath.

Percy Wrightson appeared in the doorway, wearing only his pyjama trousers. His ribs looked like tram-lines.

"What the heck—" he began, and then saw Rollison's face, and caught sight of Sammy. "Blimey!" he burst out.

Brrr-brrr.

"Take him in the bathroom and douse him with cold water," Rollison said, huskily. He shook out his handkerchief and dabbed his mouth; a crimson stain spread over the white linen. He picked up the telephone and announced: "Rollison?" as Wrightson took Sammy by the arm and led him away.

"Mr. Grice for you. Hold on."

Rollison dabbed at his lips again and moved his tongue about the inside of his mouth gingerly. His eyes were watering and his ear was stinging; he must look a sight, too. Whenever he moistened his lips there was the sharp tang of blood on them.

"Rolly," Grice was brusque.

"Yes, Bill?"

"I asked you to ring me as soon as you were in, and you've been back for twenty minutes."

"Yes, Bill."

"If you go on like this you'll have a head-on clash with us."

"I certainly will if you go on in this way," Rollison said. "I haven't telephoned you because I've had too much to do."

"You mean you've been talking to Slimm."

"Talking is one word," Rollison said, ruefully. "Just now I'm nursing two loosened teeth and a black eye and possibly a cracked jaw-bone all handed out by Sammy Slimm because I wouldn't storm into the Yard and demand that you let him see Marta Estino. Don't drive me too hard, Bill. I could lose my temper."

"Oh," said Grice sounding much more mild. "Like that, is it. Are you all right?"

"Can't you hear the plum in my mouth?"

"I thought it was your tongue in your cheek," said Grice. "Rolly, listen to me. I think you might be in very real danger, and I think that you could be very wrong to trust Slimm. Can I have your assurance that nothing I say to you will be passed on to him?"

"Yes."

"Not even by implication?"

"In no way at all," said Rollison, and added hastily: "That is, if it's something different from what I've already told him. I said that you almost certainly knew that he had doped Marta this afternoon, and that if so you would take it for granted that he did it to make sure that she couldn't talk to any policeman."

Grice said heavily: "So you knew she'd been drugged?"

"Yes."

"Why didn't you tell—" began Grice. Then he seemed to move farther away from the telephone, and say: "Oh, forget it. There is something else which makes things look very black against Slimm. If you tell him what it is he might decide to cut and run, and if he should do, we would have to detain and charge him. That's why it's essential that you shouldn't tell him anything. We don't want to have to charge him yet."

"Charge him with what, Bill?"

Grice said, very deliberately: "With the murder of Professor Estino."

Rollison didn't speak.

"So you're as shocked as that, are you?" Grice said.

"Could you make a charge and have any hope of holding him?" asked Rollison, but he felt quite sure that Grice wouldn't go this far unless he was really confident.

"Yes. His fingerprints have been found at *Faraway*, in the room where Estino was staying, and where blood from Group O – Professor Estino's group – has been found. The bullet taken out of the wardrobe was fired from the .22 gun which was used to kill Estino."

"Well, well," said Rollison, heavily. "That begins to add up, Bill."

"Yes."

"When you asked Sammy Slinun to help in this case, did you know that he might be involved?" Grice didn't answer.

"Now who's holding out on whom?" asked Rollison, wryly. He felt almost certain that Grice had wanted Slimm to be drawn into the case. If that were so he must have had some reason for suspecting him. There had been no coincidence, only the appearance of one, so Grice had certainly not confided in him, Rollison, very fully. It was understandable enough if Grice had wanted to use him so that he could bring influence to bear on Sammy; and it was characteristic of Grice's cunning.

"Yes, I knew that he might know something," Grice admitted as if grudgingly.

"Don't tell me you knew who the victim was," Rollison said, almost fearfully.

"We didn't know that until he came and told us," said Grice. "But one of our men on Hampstead Heath saw him on the night that Estino's body was found. Slimm is unmistakable. When I realised he might be involved I thought it would be a good idea to draw him closer into the affair. He came in readily. You don't need more telling that he's involved, do you?"

"No."

"Or why we're keeping him a long way from that girl," went on Grice. "If I'd dreamed that he would do what he did to her this afternoon I would have made sure that he couldn't get within a mile of her. I thought that it might be possible to make him talk to you when he wasn't likely to talk to us. And that's your job, now. You've got to find out what he knows and what this is all about. At the moment I could bring him in. By the time we produce the bullet, prove that he was at *Faraway* and also prove that he was seen on Hampstead Heath on the night the body was left there, it would make a very strong case against him."

After a pause, Rollison said: "Why aren't you charging him? You often charge a man on much less evidence than this."

"I don't think it's the right moment," Grice replied. "I doubt if he's in this alone. I think if he's free to move about and make contacts he might lead us to his associates."

"The Bells of Wimbledon?"

"I don't know yet, but it's possible. Obviously they could have known what was going to happen, and could have got out of the country so that it could take place while they were away, leaving them in the clear. Rolly, I'm relying on your judgement as a responsible citizen to help us, not to help Slimm."

"I'll help just one thing," Rollison said softly. "To find out the truth."

"That's what I want to hear."

"Thanks, Bill," said Rollison. "Any trace of the Bells' servants?"

"None at all," said Grice at once. "We have discovered one thing that's interesting, though."

"What's that?"

"They haven't obtained a Spanish visa recently, so they haven't gone home."

"There are still a lot of places where they could have gone," remarked Rollison. "Now before you ring off, what can you tell me about a motive?"

"Slimm's, you mean?"

"Yes."

Rollison was now aware of movement in the doorway leading from the domestic quarters and he shifted his position so that he could see. Sammy and Wrightson stood there. Sammy's hair was like a golliwog's, obviously it had been drenched and rough dried, but his clothes seemed dry, so Wrightson had done a neat as well as a good job. Sammy looked dazed and almost calm. Wrightson had a hand on his wrist, obviously to make sure that he could not come in unless Rollison approved.

Rollison nodded at them.

Grice was saying: "Nothing, Rolly. That's one of our missing links. But we can find the motive later if we can prove the case. Or you can find it for us."

"Another of my jobs," said Rollison, heavily. "All right, Bill. Thanks." He rang off, as Sammy advanced into the room. He had no time to think, no time to adjust himself from one situation to another – that was in some ways the worst feature of this case. He had to wrench his mind off Grice and concentrate on Sammy – and make sure he didn't let any incautious word drop.

The almost pathetic thing about Sammy was that he was near tears. They shimmered on his eyes. His hands were shaking too, and Rollison knew that above everything else Sammy wanted what he himself had given Marta Estino: a deep sleep.

Sammy could have killed Dr. Estino. Moreover, he had a motive which Grice knew nothing about. But was it a motive which would explain everything that had happened? Was he simply in love with Marta Estino? If he was, if everything he had done had been due to that, would he have employed Max Cato to try to kill her?

That made no sense at all.

There was a chance that in his present shivery, remorseful mood and with his nerves so raw, Sammy might talk freely. It was late and Rollison was tired and would have to be busy early next morning, but obviously his next job was to try to act as father confessor.

Chapter Seventeen

Confessional?

"What did he want?" asked Sammy in a subdued voice. Did he tell you he suspected me?"

"He told me that he wasn't satisfied that you've yet told him all you know," replied Rollison. "Have you, Sammy?" He beckoned to Percy, who was hovering in the doorway, obviously hoping that he would be able to overhear a great deal. "Ever warmed milk, Percy?"

"*Milk*, Mr. Ar? My wife has a glass've hot milk every day of her life. Drinka pinta milka day, don't they say? How many?"

"Just one – unless you'd like one."

Wrightson gave a polite shudder. "Won't be long," he promised.

Sammy now dropped into a chair. His eyes were heavy and yet bright with that suspicion of unshed tears. His lips kept twitching, as if he couldn't control the nerves of his face. He folded his hands in front of him, locking the fingers tightly.

"How much do you know, Sammy?" asked Rollison.

"Can I—can I trust you not to tell the police?"

Very deliberately, Rollison said: "Not if I think they ought to know."

"You don't help much, do you?" There was reproach, but little bitterness in Sammy's voice.

"I don't necessarily agree with the police about what they think they ought to know," Rollison remarked. "If I think it would serve the ends of justice best by keeping material facts from them, I'll keep 'em. They don't eat out of my hand and I don't eat out of theirs. I'll keep anything you say in confidence if I think it's the best way to find out what really happened, to help you and to help Marta. But Sammy, don't let's have any misunderstanding. If you killed Estino, I can't save you from the consequences. A barrister might, but that's not my job. If there are extenuating circumstances that's for judge and jury to pronounce on, not for me."

Sammy said: "You really think I killed him, don't you?"

"I think you had the chance, and you've already told me that you had a motive."

Sammy gulped. "I had a motive all right. And I had the chance. Rolly, I—I suppose I'll have to tell you now, but I don't think the police ought to know. I really don't. They'd be bound to arrest me, and then I wouldn't have a chance to help Marta. She's all I can think about. It's a strange thing," he went on chokily, "I'd never paid much attention to women before. Not so far as marriage was concerned, anyhow. I had one or two mild affairs, and now and again I went on the tiles, but—I'm forty-one, Rolly. Until I met Marta I'd never been in love. Not this kind of all-obsessional love, anyhow. It drives out thought of everything else, seems to burn me right up. I suppose you've never known what it's like."

"Just assume that I know," said Rollison, gently.

Sammy frowned. "I wonder if—oh, forget it. Well, I'll tell you the simple truth. I wanted Marta to marry me, but her father laughed me off. She was too valuable to him. She did everything he wanted, she was virtually a slave. He couldn't have managed without her and knew it. He—he was a clever man, a brilliant biologist and a great humanitarian in nearly every way, but his attitude to Marta was wickedly possessive."

Sammy paused, but Rollison made no comment, so Sammy went on: "Not long ago I heard they were coming over to London. In our line of business these days there's a lot of gossip. Television has made a big difference, you know. It leaked out in Portugal that Estino was planning another expedition, and a newspaper got hold of the story and telephoned me and asked if I had any plans to meet him or go with him. They said they wondered, because we'd met on the last expedition. I told them the truth, that I knew nothing at all about it. But I soon discovered where they were going to stay."

"Where?"

"A house in Wimbledon, with another family who go out on these expeditions. Some people named Bell." Obviously Sammy had not the slightest idea where Rollison had been that night. "I've met them, they're a nice enough family as far as I know. They've got a rather pretty daughter. Anyhow, I went over to Wimbledon. I didn't say I was going because the Bells would have told Estino, and he would have kept me away from Marta. He might even have forbidden her to see me. I thought if I caught them all on the hop I'd have a chance to see her and I might be able to reason with Estino. I got there about seven o'clock in the evening. The Bells weren't there. A couple of Spanish servants were in charge, and Estino and Marta were staying as their guests. I thought it a bit odd, but didn't worry much about it, what arrangements the Bells made with their servants was no concern of mine. They took me up to Estino's room. I pleaded, but got nowhere. He simply told me to get out. He wouldn't even let me see Marta. She was actually in the next room, but he wouldn't let me see her. And I wouldn't go. We had a dreadful row. You know what I'm like when I get mad, and was I mad!"

Sammy screwed up his eyes.

"Did you hit him, Sammy?"

"I could have broken his neck."

"Did you *hit* him?"

"I couldn't," said Sammy, miserably. "He was twenty years older than I. I couldn't knock him about like I tried to you, could I? It was just a shouting match, really. I told him what I would do to him if he didn't change his mind, I threatened everything under the sun from simple murder to hanging, drawing and quartering. Oh, God, I was like a madman. All he did was to stand and stare at me. Occasionally he would say something quietly. Venomously – but quietly. If it hadn't been for Marta, I think I *would* have hit him. She got out of the room she was in – the servants must have unlocked the door – and pleaded with me to leave. So in the end I left. That's all – I just left. But think what this would look like to the police. Just think."

"I've been thinking," Rollison said, quietly.

"They'd think I killed him, wouldn't they?'

"They might. Did you take a gun with you, Sammy?"

Sammy didn't answer, but his jaw dropped.

"Did you?" persisted Rollison. He hoped against hope that the answer would be no, or that if it were yes then Sammy Slimm had taken a gun which was not a .22. "Let's have the whole truth, Sammy. Did you take a gun?"

Sammy's eyes were screwed up and his forehead wrinkled as if he were in pain.

"Yes."

"What kind of gun?"

"A—a .22 automatic pistol," Sammy muttered. Rollison was glad that his eyes were still closed so that he couldn't see his, Rollison's, expression. "I actually took it out of my pocket and threatened Estino with it. I tried so hard to make him give in. Can't you understand how I felt? He'd *locked* Marta away from me. He behaved as if he owned her, body and soul. I just had to try to break him down."

"By shooting him?" asked Rollison coldly.

"No," said Sammy, heavily. At last he opened his eyes. There was calmness in them now, as if telling this story had helped to ease away his tension. "No," he said in a low-pitched voice. "Marta took the gun away from me. She defied her father and left the room with me. We had half an hour together before I left. She told me that she couldn't leave him, that it was useless to fight, that no matter how much she loved me her first duty must always be to him. She came out with me, Rolly. Just for a while. We walked about the Common until she tore herself away. It wasn't until I was half-way back to my place that I realised that I'd left the gun on the desk in Estino's room. I suppose it was the gun which was used to kill him. Do you know if that was a .22?"

Rollison told him, quietly, that he did know. Wrightson, who had heard much of this story while standing motionless with a glass of milk in his hand, turned away when Rollison motioned to him. He returned in a few minutes with the milk heated up. Rollison went into his bedroom, took out some veronal capsules which he used for emergencies, came back and held them out to Sammy on the palm of his hand.

"You must have a good night," he said. "Don't argue. If you're dopey in the morning the police won't be able to question you, will they? I certainly won't tell them this until I've had a chance to talk it over with you again."

Quite meekly, Sammy swallowed the capsules. Nothing could have been greater proof that he was at the point of exhaustion. Ten minutes later he was dozing off in the spare-room bed.

"Don't misunderstand me, Mr. Ar," said Wrightson, later, "but I always thought the life of a gentlemen's gentleman was full of comfort and ease. And I thought the gentleman hisself—" He broke off. "You've got to be pretty tough to stand the pace, aincha?"

"Pretty tough, Percy."

"Think Sammy did it?"

"Who?"

"Sam—I mean the Perfessor," corrected Wrightson, standing almost to attention.

"That's what we're going to find out," said Rollison. He glanced at his wristwatch. "Half past three, is it? Bring me some tea at seven o'clock sharp, Percy, will you? I want to be over at Bill Ebbutt's place by eight."

For the first time in Rollison's experience Percy Wrightson was absolutely at a loss for words.

Yet at seven o'clock next morning, as the alarm clock by Rollison's side began to ring, there was a tap at the door. Percy came in, fully dressed, but not yet shaven. He carried a tea-tray and placed it by Rollison's side, then picked up the milk jug and began to pour out. Rollison struggled up to a sitting position, yawned and gratefully accepted a cup of tea.

"Nice morning," remarked Wrightson brightly. "The Perfessor is still sleeping the sleep of the—well, come to think we don't know whether he is just or not, do we? Any breakfast before you go, Mr. Ar?"

"Telephone Bill and ask him if I can have breakfast with him," said Rollison.

He was at the Blue Dog at five minutes to eight. London's East End was in a great bustle, the meat market at Aldgate was swarming with people, porters and trucks. Carts and barrows laden with fruit and vegetables were being driven or trundled about, most of them having come straight from Covent Garden. Ebbutt's Salvation Army wife, small, sharp-featured, pert, generous and fastidious, was in the kitchen, and bacon, eggs, tomatoes and sausages were already sizzling on a gas stove. Bill came down looking enormous. His lips were puffy and sore, but otherwise he showed no signs of Cato's attack. Nothing was said about Cellar 3 or the investigation while Lil Ebbutt was bustling about, but as soon as she left them Ebbutt spoke in his wheezy rattle.

"Cato's come round, Mr. Ar. He tells me just the same yarn as he did yesterday. I can't get another word out of him." He rubbed the clean blade of his knife on a table-napkin, and halved a plump, browned sausage. "He's getting a bit restive, I would say."

"I suppose he is," said Rollison, reasoningly.

"I let him out long enough to go to the bathroom and have a shave with me electric razor," Ebbutt went on. "He's got nothing to complain about, really."

Cato, freshly-shaved, looking rested, hiding his fear with a gloss of confidence stared at Rollison as he entered Cellar 3. Before Rollison could speak he said truculently: "When are you going to let me out of here?"

"Whenever you like. The police would welcome you with open arms," said Rollison, promptly.

"You wouldn't turn me over to them, not after keeping me here and doping me," jeered Cato. "You wouldn't have the nerve. It would be as much as your reputation's worth."

Rollison looked at him coldly.

"One more crack like that, or one refusal to answer questions, and I'll send for the nearest copper," he said flatly. "I'll give evidence at your trial about exactly what I did to you and why I did it."

Cato moistened his lips, as if he realised that was no idle threat.

"I've told you everything I can," he muttered. "Aren't you satisfied?"

"Tell me again. Who sent you to kill Marta Estino?"

"Matheson Bell did – I've *told* you."

"Who actually shot Estino?"

"I don't know. I think it was Bell, but I don't know."

"Did you see Bell at the house about the time of the shooting?"

"Of course I did! I've told you all I know already. He made me take the body over to Hampstead. He knew I was terrified of those bloody spiders and snakes he keeps there. Once I tried to back out of a job he wanted me to do, and he took me up there and threatened to lock me in." Cato's forehead glistened with perspiration and he kept licking his lips. "It was Bell, who else do you think it was if it wasn't Bell?"

"Did you see anyone else there?"

"I've seen plenty of people there, but I didn't see anyone this time, except the servants. Lopez, their name is, Miguel and Anita Lopez. Bell's got them where he wants them just as he has me. Bell's the man you want."

"Would you say so in court?"

Cato hesitated. "If I knew he was going to be found guilty I would, but I wouldn't want to give evidence if he was going to be set free. He'd come after me. He'd get me, too. Don't make any mistake about Bell, he's a devil. And don't let his wife and daughter fool you, either. They're just as bad as he is. They talk and look as if they go to church once a day and twice on Sundays, but they're she-cats. Don't let them fool you, Rollison. And be careful. If they know you're gunning for them they'll get you somehow."

Chapter Eighteen

Marta Remembers

Rollison pulled his Bentley into the approach to New Scotland Yard, was saluted as if he were a V.I.P. of the Metropolitan Police Force and was allowed to go alone to Grice's office. It was half past nine. The Yard looked, as always, completely under control. There was no rush, no tear, no noise; it was almost like a seminary. Rollison tapped at Grice's door. Grice called "come in" and turned round from the window. He looked fresh and rested, and nothing suggested that he had been up until the small hours.

"Morning, Rolly."

"Hallo, Bill."

"Come with the full story at last?"

"I still don't want my informant about *Faraway* to be named, but I'd like to make sure that you're checking on the Bell family."

"We're checking them all," replied Grice drily. "We won't leave anything alone that even smells of a clue. I can tell you one thing. The Bells came back from Paris in a private plane. They often charter their own. Bell is an ex-Battle of Britain pilot. The wife and daughter can fly a plane, too, they both have their pilot's licences."

"That's a help," Rollison said. "It explains why they didn't see a newspaper until they got home last night. Not everyone believes in them, Bill. Some people think they're a murderous trio."

"Nothing would surprise me," said Grice sententiously. "If they are, we'll find out"

"Anything about the Lopezes?"

"Nothing." Grice glanced down at a report in his desk. "But we've confirmed that those tram tickets were used in Lisbon on Monday morning this week, so we know more or less when the Estinos left Portugal, particularly as Marta Estino's fingerprints are on the ticket. The blood Group O is confirmed by our morning laboratory squad, too. What about your friend Slimm?"

Rollison said: "He had a wild quarrel with Estino the night that Estino was killed. He threatened to kill him. He hated him because he kept such a tight hold on his daughter. May I be present when Marta is questioned?" requested Rollison, soberly. "Then I can see how her story squares with Sammy's. If there are any discrepancies, I'll tell you."

"I suppose I can't complain, we wouldn't have gone to *Faraway*, but for you," Grice conceded. "Yes, you can be there. I've talked to Lady Gloria and Miss Lister this morning. Marta's conscious and seems much more normal. She is talking naturally and has had a light breakfast. Her doctor – or Lady Gloria's doctor, Halliday – thinks that she's over the worst of the shock. He doesn't want her to be put through too much questioning, though."

"Just enough, I hope," said Rollison.

When he went to see Marta an hour later, she was up and dressed, and sitting in Lady Gloria's private sitting-room. She wore the white pleated skirt and the off-white jumper, set more decorously at the neck now. Her hair was nicely groomed, and her complexion was flawless, but the thing which Rollison welcomed most was the calmness of her eyes. As he studied her he thought of the anguish which Sammy Slimm appeared to have suffered for this girl. He sensed how easy it would be to lose one's head over her, too. She wasn't beautiful feature by feature, but that purity of complexion and the beauty of her eyes suggested a kind of virginity that a man might well worship.

The Home Office psychologist was Dr. Nuneaton, youthful, sandy-haired, pleasant-faced, a man with a merry smile and the nearest thing to a truly appealing bedside manner Rollison had encountered for some time. He behaved with such complete naturalness that it was easy to believe that he could convince his patients that he was their friend.

"We know that you've had a very difficult time, Miss Estino, and we know what a terrible loss you've suffered. We're anxious only to make things as easy for you as we can. Will you try to help us?"

She was looking straight at him.

"I will try," she promised.

"And you know that some of the questions will have to be painful, don't you?"

"I know very well."

"Will you tell us exactly what happened from the time you reached the house called *Faraway* – Mr. Bell's house?" asked Nuneaton.

She told them: that they had been flown from Portugal by a man named Cato, an Englishman whom she had met in the Far East on her last expedition with her father. There was some reason for secrecy, but she did not know what it was. Her father had talked to Bell by telephone and decided to leave for London at once. She was so used to doing whatever he said that it had not occurred to her to ask why they should not fly by an ordinary service. In any case, in remote parts of the world they flew by small aircraft and sometimes chartered their own so there was nothing remarkable about this flight.

"Did you see Mr. Bell or his family when you arrived?" the doctor asked.

Rollison waited almost breathlessly for the answer. Marta did not leave him in suspense.

"No," she said simply.

"Whom did you see?"

"The servants, Miguel and Anita."

"Did you know them well?"

"Sometimes we had met, yes, when we had come to see Mr. Bell and his family in London."

"So you had been to that house before?"

"Oh, yes. Sometimes to compare notes, sometimes to exchange specimens. You see, we supplied many zoos and biological schools all over the world. Sometimes we would receive an order for some specimen – perhaps a snake, a monkey, a spider, a bird, a butterfly, anything which was small and which we did not have. So we would find out who else would have what we wanted, and so help our clients. Is that not reasonable?"

"It's very reasonable indeed," Nuneaton assured her. "So you saw only the servants?"

"When we arrived there, yes."

"Did you see anyone else at all?"

"Yes, of course, I saw Professor Slimm."

Grice, on the far side of the room, taking notes, glanced sharply at Rollison. The girl was speaking with complete self-possession, and if it were possible to judge from her manner she had nothing at all to hide. Could such simplicity be entirely genuine? Wasn't it at least as likely that this was a carefully rehearsed story? Had there been a chance for her to be primed by anyone since she had been held by the police?

"Why was Professor Slimm there?" asked Nuneaton.

Marta did not smile, but it was possible to imagine that her expression softened.

"He came to see me, only. My father did not wish it. I am afraid there was a quarrel. After a while, I went to try to stop them from quarrelling so angrily. I believe that I succeeded. I went out with Professor Slimm for a while, because he was in such distress. I returned to the house and went straight to my room."

That was the moment when Rollison would have let her go on in full flood – and that was the moment when Nuneaton interrupted her.

"Why didn't you go to your father, Miss Estino? Were you on bad terms with him?"

"Bad terms – no, of course not! It is not always possible for father and daughter to wish to do the same things, I fully understood that. But he was in his room, alone, and had he wished to see me he would have left the door open or would have sent a message. I know that he was very angry with Professor Slimm and he would not wish to discuss him with me. I was reading in my room when—when I heard the shot." She closed her eyes, and reminded Rollison of the way Sammy Slimm looked when he was talking about something which he disliked. "I heard two shots," she repeated in a low-pitched voice, "I ran out to see what had happened, and I found my father in his room. In his room—*dead."*

Rollison could not fail to see her tension. He remembered how the shock had affected her, hoped that Nuneaton would not press her too far now. But Nuneaton did. He took her hands, looked straight into her eyes, and asked: "What did you do?"

She began to speak quickly, breathlessly.

"I can remember screaming, that is all. I can remember screaming! And then I heard Anita scream, too. That is all I can remember until I woke up here. *It is all I can remember.* It was as if a great black cloud smothered me and I could not see or hear until I woke in the room in this house. That is all I can remember."

She was quivering.

Nuneaton said gently: "Did you see anyone in your father's room?"

"No."

"Do you know who fired the shots?"

"No."

"How many shots were there?"

"Please, I do not wish—"

"How many shots were there?"

"Two," she said, gaspingly. "Two, that is all."

"Did you see anyone at all until after you heard the shots?"

"I—I do not understand you."

It was clumsy questioning, Rollison thought angrily. He wished he could find a way of stopping Nuneaton. Yet at the back of his mind he realised that the psychiatrist was trying to make sure that she buried nothing in her subconscious. He was trying to make sure that she talked fully about the horror so that it should not he dormant in her, and fester, and become a sore on her mind.

"After you returned to the house did you see anyone until you saw your father?"

"No, I did not."

"Are you sure?"

"Of course I am sure!"

"Do you know who shot your father?" Nuneaton asked. "If you know, you must tell us. Did you see him?"

"No!" she cried.

"Are you sure you're telling the truth?"

"Yes, yes." Marta turned to Maggie, who was sitting by her side, and there was desperation as well as fear in her eyes. "Please make him stop these questions. They are so many, I cannot answer any more."

"You must tell all the truth," Nuneaton insisted. He released her hand and stood back. He looked grave, and older than when he had first come in. His voice had a curious clarity, was almost bell-like. "Did you see the gun with which your father was shot?"

"Please—"

"Did you see it?"

She cried: "I saw a gun, but I do not believe that it killed my father. I tell you I do not believe it! He was trying to frighten him, that is all. He was trying to make him change his mind about me."

"Who was this man you call 'he'?" asked Nuneaton.

"I have told you. It was Professor Slimm. It must have been his gun. I heard him threaten my father with it. But it was only to frighten him, he would not have killed him. I went away with him, I saw him go, I tell you it could not have been Professor Slimm."

"Where was the gun you saw?" asked Nuneaton evenly.

She screwed up her eyes again and said in a trembling voice: "It was in my father's room. It was Professor Slimm's gun. But I am sure he did not use it. I tell you I am sure."

There was a curiously disarming naturalness about what followed. Maggie and Lady Gloria took over in the sitting-room, Nuneaton, Grice and Rollison went into Maggie's office, across the hall, where a pleasant-faced woman brought coffee and biscuits. Grice scanned through the shorthand notes he had made; it looked as if he had managed to get everything down *verbatim*. Rollison did not speak to him. Nuneaton talked casually and rather pointlessly until Grice put his notes down, and said: "How does it square with what Slimm told you, Rolly?"

"In nearly every detail."

"He could easily have come back and killed Estino."

"Oh, yes." Rollison sipped his coffee. "There couldn't be any possibility of suicide, could there?"

"None at all," Grice replied with such assurance that Rollison gave the idea up immediately. "I shall have to bring Professor Slimm in, of course, and charge him. You know that, don't you? Would you rather I sent for him before you go back?"

"No," said Rollison, slowly. "No, Bill. I'll go and tell him what's happened, and I'll tell him that the reason for the charge against him is the statement of his precious Marta. It will hit him very hard. Give me time to handle him, won't you?"

"I shall have to have men at the back and front of your flat to make sure that he doesn't escape," Grice warned.

"You do that," said Rollison, heavily. He expected Grice to press him again to say how he had learned about *Faraway*. He still did not want to give Cato up, for the prisoner might yet be the key to the puzzle – if it was a puzzle any longer. One possibility had to be faced: that Sammy had employed Cato, that Sammy had paid him to name Matheson Bell and his family, that in spite of his protestations of love Sammy had wanted Marta dead and had paid Cato to kill her, so that she could not tell the truth about him.

Once he had realised that there was no way of preventing the police from questioning her and finding out the truth, he might have decided that he must tell Rollison exactly what had happened, so that the story came first from him and not from Marta.

Yes, Sammy Slimm could be the murderer, but for what reason? The only motive that Rollison knew did not square with what had followed the death of Estino.

"I'd like you to go and get this over with Slimm as soon as you can," Grice said.

"Right!" Rollison stood up promptly. "There is one other thing worth remembering, Bill."

"What's that?"

"If Marta didn't see the actual murder, then the attack on her might have been for a different motive from anything we yet know."

"Possibly," said Grice, and added drily: "There's one thing you might do well to remember, too."

"What's that?"

"Marta Estino might be lying for Slimm's sake. She might be as deeply in love with him as he appears to be with her. This might be a murder which he committed and to which she was accessory. The actual crime might easily have shocked her into the condition she was in when we found her wandering about in the West End."

"I suppose it could," agreed Rollison, non-committally.

He shook hands with Nuneaton and left the Marigold Club without seeing Maggie or Lady Gloria. He had come by taxi and had to walk for five minutes before he caught one for Gresham Terrace. Outside the house where he had his flat were two plain-clothes men and he was quite sure that there would be others at the back. The police were quite determined not to give Sammy a chance to escape.

Now he, Rollison, had to go and tell Sammy just how bad the news was; and how quickly Marta had been persuaded to cast ugly suspicion on him.

The worst of it was that he could not convince himself that Sammy was innocent, but as he went upstairs he realised how desperately he wanted him to be.

Chapter Nineteen

Arrest

"She couldn't have told them," Sammy said in a choky voice. "She couldn't have done it."

"She's not really herself," Rollison tried to soothe him. "And it's only what you told me, Sammy. In the long run it's best that it should come out."

Sammy stared, his eyes taking on that familiar hard glitter, as if there were a sheen of hate in them.

"We'll have you out of this before long," Rollison went on. "I'll arrange for a good lawyer, and—"

"I don't believe Marta told the police this."

"She did, Sammy. I was there."

"I don't believe it," Sammy repeated doggedly. "I think you told them, and that you're blaming her. You're trying to destroy everything that's wonderful between us. Why I ought to break your neck."

Rollison waited, warily. Nothing would surprise him, and he knew enough of Sammy Slimm's wiry strength and fighting ability to know that he would want a lot of beating. He felt a sense of irritation, almost of exasperation, mixed with doubt. Would an innocent man really behave like this? Wasn't Sammy twisting and turning to try to avoid the consequences of a crime which he had himself committed?

"Tell me the truth." The reedy voice was pitched higher than Rollison had ever known it. "You told the police this, didn't you? Then you put the words in Marta's mouth. She wouldn't have told them. I know she wouldn't."

"If she'd been herself she wouldn't."

"She was herself! Why, you—"

As he came forward Rollison hit him in the solar plexus with all the force he could muster; this had to be over quickly. He flashed an uppercut to the chin as Sammy jerked forward. Sammy reeled back a few feet, then flopped down like a log. Percy Wrightson appeared as if from nowhere. He went down on one knee beside Sammy, pulled up his eyelids, turned and looked up at Rollison with unfeigned admiration.

"You still pack a punch, Mr. Ar, don't you? What's got into him, though? Can you understand the perisher?"

"I wish I did," said Rollison. But he was more than ever afraid. If Sammy was guilty, then it was easy to understand. *If only he knew the real motive.* Heavy hearted, he went to the window and beckoned. Immediately two of Grice's men moved across the road. By the time they were in the flat Sammy was coming round. He was dazed and shocked. Percy supported him while a detective sergeant made the charge in brisk, dispassionate voice. Sammy hardly seemed to understand.

"And anything you say may be used in evidence," the sergeant said. "Come along, sir, please."

Sammy didn't speak, but he glared at Rollison with such malevolence that when the door was closed on him, Percy Wrightson said in a subdued voice: "You ever done anything to make the Perfessor hate you, Mr. Ar?"

"Not that I know of, Percy."

"Well, hate's the word."

"It certainly looks like it."

"And there's another thing," said Percy, "if you won't take no offence if I mention it."

"I won't take offence."

"The guy who put those snakes and those spiders in your flat didn't exactly love you, did he? That's the kind of thing people do if they hate your guts. There are lots of ways of lulling a man without using that kind of poison. Sure nothing happened between you and the Perfessor before this malarky started?"

"Yes, I'm sure," said Rollison.

He was as sure as he could be, but as he went to his desk and began to look through correspondence which had accumulated in the past two days, he realised that there might be some hidden factor of which he knew nothing. The possibility that Sammy Slimm had hated him enough to send the snakes and the spiders still seemed ridiculous, but this fresh doubt was very strong. It was like a poison, as venomous as from any snake. It was the first time he could remember working for a man in whom he did not believe absolutely.

He finished the correspondence, then telephoned the hospital. Jolly was still improving, and officially was "quite comfortable." Normally Rollison would have gone to see him, but in this mood he would start talking too freely and that wouldn't help Jolly to get better. The disadvantage of having no one with whom to discuss the case had seldom been so great. He sat at his desk and read through the newspaper cuttings, then made notes, then pondered over everything he knew and had heard. Certain inescapable facts emerged: Cato could be lying. If he wasn't, then the Bell family was treacherous and deadly – and it was almost impossible to believe that of all three.

If Cato was lying, then he might be attempting to save Sammy Slimm. This possibility would be strengthened if he could find a connection between Cato and Sammy. If one existed, it would look even uglier against Sammy.

Cato had fired at Marta with the gun which had killed her father. But if Sammy had committed the murder of Estino and Cato was working with him, then it would have been easy to pass the gun on.

It might now be time to hand Cato over to the police. They would be able to check more thoroughly, and would find it much easier to discover whether he had any close association with Sammy. As he had a pilot's certificate and knew the Far East well, he might have piloted Sammy as well as Estino and the Bells. A stubborn streak made Rollison reluctant to turn Cato over to the police yet, however; he still felt that it might be possible to frighten the man into telling the truth. He ought to have at least one more try. The moment the decision was made he felt better. He was actually at the door, ready to go downstairs, and Ebbutt had been warned to expect him, when the telephone bell rang.

Percy answered it and soon bellowed: "It's the Super, skipper!"

Rollison, in a brighter mood, grinned to himself and went to speak to Grice, expecting to find him thoroughly amiable now that he had held Sammy. Instead, Rollison sensed the moment he heard Grice's voice that all was not well.

"You only just caught me, Bill."

"It's as well for you that I did," said Grice. "Now listen to me. I'm telephoning from a call-box because I don't want anyone at the Yard to know what a fool I can make myself. I've heard that Ebbutt is holding a prisoner at the Blue Dog. It's a squeal which might or might not be true, but if the Divisional men go there and find this man, and if he's concerned with the Estino murder, then you'll be really in trouble. I *mean* trouble."

Rollison said mildly: "Yes, I would be, wouldn't I? Thanks for ringing, Bill."

"Don't make light of this."

"*Light* of it?" echoed Rollison, and then contrariwise his heart lifted. "My dear chap – I'll never forget the tip! Thanks more than I can say." He rang off, held the platform for a moment, then dialled Ebbutt's number again. Ebbutt's wheezy rumble preceded him: "I thought you was on the way here, Mr. Ar."

"Later" said Rollison. "Bill, the police are coming to look for a prisoner at the Blue Dog. Get Cato out, quick. I shouldn't try to take him off the premises. Take him into the gymnasium, make him change in boxing kit and put him through some P.T. exercises. Have you got a class this morning?"

"Ten of the very best boys," said Ebbutt. "Okay, Mr. Ar. What about you?"

"I'll be over as soon as the police have realised their awful mistake," said Rollison.

He was still in a more buoyant mood when he rang off, but knew that it would not take much to dispel it. But for Grice he and Ebbutt would have been in serious trouble indeed. He could rely on Ebbutt covering up, and Cato would certainly co-operate once he realised that it was that or arrest. The odd thing was that until Grice had called Rollison had not seen the obvious thing to do with Cato. He saw it now.

An hour later he telephoned the Yard.

"Anything to report, Bill?" he asked Grice.

"No," said Grice. "You can move fast when you have to."

"Has Sammy Slimm talked to the lawyer?"

"Yes."

"Any word about those Spanish servants?"

"Nothing at all" Grice said. "I've had a note from Wimbledon – everything seems normal at *Faraway*. We know for certain that Mrs. Bell and her daughter were in Paris, and also that Bell himself was in Paris for a few hours on Monday and came back with them yesterday afternoon, but that doesn't prove he didn't slip over and land somewhere the previous night. There's no way of being certain that small aircraft don't cross the channel, land a passenger and fly straight back to France. It was cloudy on Monday and Tuesday, too."

"What about this Hollywood television agent?"

"I've got two men making inquiries of all the television and film people in London, and so far no one had any knowledge of a man named Bryer. If that's a lie, then Bell's in trouble."

"Yes," said Rollison. "Yes, he certainly is. Any objection if I go over and see the Bells later in the evening?"

"Please yourself," Grice said. "But don't play any more fool tricks."

"As if I would," said Rollison, and rang off.

He went off in the Bentley soon afterwards. It was a little after seven o'clock and traffic was light. He noticed two or three of the Divisional police near the approaches to Ebbutt's gymnasium and the Blue Dog, but no one made any attempt to speak to him. He drew up outside the gymnasium, where there was a remarkable assortment of very old cars, one or two new sports cars, motor-scooters, motorcycles and ordinary cycles. Half a dozen elderly retainers of the gymnasium were sunning themselves outside. As Rollison went inside, he heard the thudding noises of a physical training class in action. A man was calling:

"One—er—two—er—three—er—four. One—er—two—er—three—er—four," over and over again. A class of at least a dozen men of all shapes and sizes were going through ordinary exercises, arms up, arms bend, arms forward, arms bend. Over in a corner two men were doing gymnastic tricks on parallel bars, in another corner Willie was skipping with unrelenting concentration, as if his very life depended on it. Four boxers, all lightweights, were sparring in the last two rings. Ebbutt was in one corner, laying down the law. There was the odour of sawdust, sweat, canvas and massage oil.

Ebbutt came to the ropes and leaned across.

"He's in with the squad, Mr. Ar."

"When the rest go off, let him go with them," said Rollison. "Have some of your chaps follow him. I want to make quite sure where he goes."

"Sure it's the right thing to do?" asked Ebbutt uncertainly.

"No," said Rollison. "But I'm sure it has to be tried."

"Okay," said Ebbutt. "Watch your step."

Rollison watched as the training squad began to jump up and down, and swung into body twists and knee-bends. Cato was in the middle of the front line, between a lily-skinned Cockney and an ebony-black Jamaican. Cato's skin glistened like olive-coloured satin. He was not sweating any more than the rest, and he seemed able to do the exercises at least as freely as most of them.

Ebbutt came up to Rollison again.

"Not a bad boy, Mr. Ar. If I had him here I'd make something of him, you can be sure of that. Any idea where he's going?"

"It wouldn't surprise me to find him at Wimbledon," said Rollison. "That's where I'm going to be."

"I'll see you're protected," Ebbutt promised knowingly. "Anything else you want?"

"The old suit, cap and choker you keep here for me," said Rollison. "I'm going to change before I leave."

"I'd better make sure someone comes over to Wimbledon to look after you," Ebbutt said gloomily. "You be careful among all them snakes and things."

Chapter Twenty

Pick-Up

Rollison drove away in the Bentley, nodded to the Divisional men, who smiled amiably at him. He was quite sure that his progress would be reported to the Yard. He drove back to the West End, saw no sign that he was followed, parked near his garage and went to see the night foreman.

"Sorry, sir. I've got nothing to rent without a deposit," the foreman said. Then his big blue eyes widened. "Mr. Rollison! I didn't recognise you in those clothes. Do you really want an old wreck?"

"Yes. How about that old Vauxhall in the corner?"

"That's not an old wreck, that's my car!"

Rollison replied easily: "Then I'll be able to rely on it. You won't need it until morning, will you?"

"Bring it back whenever you like," the foreman said. "I can go home by bus." He hesitated before taking the five-pound note which Rollison handed him. "Thanks very much, Mr. Rollison. Any time you want to use it, it's yours."

Rollison drove off. The engine responded sweetly and there was real pleasure in driving a car with old-type gears. He did not think much about that, however, but took the cap out of his pocket as soon as he was out of the central London area, put it on and wound the choker round his neck. No one looking at him as he passed would have recognised the driver of the Bentley.

He went straight to Wimbledon Common, pulled in behind trees from which he could watch *Faraway* and studied the other men who were stationed at good vantage points. Grice had three officers within sight; he wasn't taking any chances with the Bells.

It was half past eight and still broad daylight. Everything seemed quite normal, even the stuttering noise of a scooter as it came along the Common road. Rollison watched the man on it and frowned. Was it Cato? His heart began to beat faster. If it was, then he had dyed his hair or was wearing a wig. As the man passed Rollison realised that it wasn't Cato; there hadn't been time for him to dye his hair or even to bleach it.

Another man came along on a scooter, and this time Rollison saw and recognised him almost with a sense of anti-climax.

This *was* Cato, bare-headed and making no attempt to disguise himself. He was driving the blue motor-scooter which he had used on the night when he had shot at Marta. He slowed down, then turned into the drive gates of *Faraway;* they were open tonight. The engine stopped. Rollison was almost opposite the house. Then he saw one of Grice's men signal to another who was in a radio car, and could imagine that a message about this visitor was being flashed to the Yard. Rollison wanted to get across to the house, but could not do so without being noticed. The best chance would be to go in one of the gardens alongside and climb a wall. Rollison left the cover of the trees, but before he stepped on to the road, the motor-scooter engine started up again. He saw one of Ebbutt's men farther along the road, fiddling with the engine of a motor-cycle; he stopped fiddling as soon as the scooter came in sight.

Cato wasn't alone. Nora Bell was on his pillion.

Ebbutt's man roared off in the wake of the couple, and winked at Rollison as he passed. Another message flashed from a watching policeman to a patrol car, but no one followed the couple. It all looked so innocent – boy calling for girl, girl waiting for him eagerly. It was the right kind of evening, too. Rollison strolled back to his car. He saw the motor-scooter on a narrow by-road leading across the Common with Ebbutt's man behind it. Rollison started to walk towards them quickly, quite sure that no one would recognise him from a distance. They weren't likely to go far; there were one or two parking spaces for picnics and one or two patches of trees and clumps of hawthorn and bramble bushes. Most couples would head for these. Not far away was the Windmill Café, but that was used more by families than by courting couples.

He saw the motor-scooter turn off the by-road, and began to hurry. Ebbutt's man did not follow the scooter, but went straight on and turned round a hundred yards or so ahead. A clump of bramble bushes hid Rollison from the couple. He waved to Ebbutt's man, who came hurrying towards him. As they met, on one side of the bush, a girl giggled.

"Oh, you," she said.

Then, she sighed.

Rollison whispered. "Leave me your motor-bike, will you?"

"Okay, Mr. Ar."

"*What's that?*" the unseen girl whispered.

"Think we're the only ones on the Common?" inquired a youth in a lazy voice.

Rollison moved away. He strolled more casually, acutely aware that some people were watching him. Men often wandered about here by night, on the look-out for a girl who had been let down and was in the mood for a pick-up. A teenager with a beautiful head of auburn hair watched Rollison, and after a while drew nearer. She didn't speak, but moved in front of him, smiling beautifully. She was as seductive a little piece as he had seen for many a long day.

He had to step round her, or bump into her. He went straight up. She didn't change her expression, but let him come breast to breast, until they almost touched. Rollison stopped.

"Hallo," she said, lifting her face to his.

"What I ought to do is put you over my knee," Rollison said. "Would you like to risk being shot?"

"I don't mind what I risk." Her green eyes laughed at him.

"I know you don't believe it, but I'm serious."

She frowned a little. "You almost sound as if you are. What are the odds?"

"Fifty-fifty."

"What happens if I come out of it alive?"

"A week out, with any restaurant you like in London every evening, or if you prefer it, a week-end in Paris."

"With *you?*"

"I'm not making any promises," Rollison said. He looked over her head, for she did not come much above his shoulder. Cato and Nora Bell were walking towards a thicket of bramble. They were talking with their heads close together, but were not arm-in-arm. "I want to get close to a couple over there without them thinking I'm spying on them."

The girl drew back for the first time. Her expression changed, she was almost angry.

"If this is a divorce case—"

"It's not." Rollison pushed past her, saying carelessly: "Please yourself, Ginger." He had not gone three steps before the girl was alongside, linking her arm through his. He glanced down at her pretty pert face, and felt a kind of sadness at the thought that a girl who looked so nice and spoke so well would thrust herself on a complete stranger. Didn't she realise the risk? He slid his arm round her waist and she nestled against him. They drew nearer the other couple. Cato glanced round, but took no notice of them. Rollison and the girl turned along a little path between some bushes, and the girl looked up into his face as if adoringly.

They came to a clearing which had obviously been many a lover's bower.

"You stay here," Rollison said, whispering into her ear. "Don't go away, and keep talking as if I'm with you. Understand?"

"You're a queer one, you are," the redhead said. "How long are you going to be?"

"Five minutes or so." Rollison gave her a squeeze. She bent her knees and sat down with a graceful movement, hugged her legs and smiled up at him.

"Don't be long," she whispered.

He grinned and moved off. Bushes and trees still concealed him from the others. Cato was talking to Nora and did not trouble to look round; he must feel quite sure that he was in no danger from the couple. Behind Rollison, the redhaired girl said in a clear, laughing voice: *"Oh, you!"*

Rollison heard Nora Bell's voice. He was quite sure that she was protesting about something, but he could not distinguish the words. He drew nearer. In a few yards he would be out of the cover of the bushes, and he dared not leave it. He strained his ears.

"You're a fast worker, aren't you?" said the redhead. He got the impression that she was enjoying this.

"But we can't," Nora said, in a tense voice.

"You'd better," said Cato.

"It's impossible."

"It wouldn't take me long to call the police," Cato threatened.

"You've already had five hundred pounds."

"I brought you out here so that I can talk some sense into you – you can get busy on your Pa and Ma. I want a thousand and I want it by the morning and if I don't get it I'll tell the police exactly what they'll find buried under the monkey-house," Cato said.

Rollison, crouching, inched farther forward. Every word, every syllable might be of importance. He actually held his breath as he listened. Probably because he was so intent on his demands Cato raised his voice a little. It still only just carried to Rollison's ears but every syllable was clear.

"You go back and talk to them, and I'll telephone at twelve o'clock sharp. Got that?"

"I tell you we haven't got that much money!"

"Well, sell your stock," said Cato. *"That's worth plenty."*

"No one would buy it at short notice."

"Who are you trying to fool?" demanded Cato. *"Slimm would buy it, wouldn't he? A lot of other people would, too. I've spent enough time here with you. I want a thousand pounds by noon tomorrow, and I'll call your father at midnight to tell him where to bring it."*

Cato turned away. The girl called out: *"Please don't."* Behind Rollison the redhead seemed to be laughing at some wicked joke. Cato strode past the bushes where Rollison was hiding. At one stage he would have seen Rollison had he looked round, but he strode straight to the motor-scooter and Rollison had time to back away. Soon, the scooter motor started up and Cato rode off. Rollison, more securely hidden, watched until Nora Bell came in sight. She looked so unhappy that it was impossible not to feel sorry for her. Her shoulders sagged and there was no spring in her walk. She stared at the ground all the time. Once she was near enough for Rollison to hear her sigh.

He turned back to the clearing. The redhead was lying on her back, with her hands behind her head, which was pillowed on a little mound of grass. She showed plenty of nicely-shaped legs, but was fully dressed. She didn't move as Rollison drew nearer, but smiled up at him and shaped her lips into a kiss.

"Ginger, you're barmy," said Rollison.

She was so startled that she sat up.

"Quite, quite barmy," Rollison went on. "With a face and figure and a complexion like that you could marry into money and live happily ever after. Every time you fool around like this you're cheapening yourself as well as everyone who fools around with you, and you're throwing away your main chance. Get up."

"Why, you pig!"

"Get up," repeated Rollison. He went forward, stretched down and gripped her hands and pulled her to her feet. "Call at Thomas Cook's in Berkeley Street tomorrow and ask for a Mr. Stanley. He'll give you your ticket to Paris and everything you need for that weekend. Have a *good* time."

She said in perplexity: "I don't get it."

"That's the trouble," Rollison said. He twisted her round and gave her a spank, then turned and went off. He reached his motor-cycle while Nora Bell was still in sight. He drove after her, passed her before she reached the road and parked the motor-cycle.

Nothing near *Faraway* had changed. He took off the choker and the cap, tossed them through the open window of the Vauxhall and walked a hundred yards along until he reached the Common road at a corner. He stepped into full sight of the policemen. They would wonder where he had come from, but would probably assume that his car was round the corner. He walked briskly along. The girl was out of sight; she would have reached home by now. He turned into the carriageway where he had been in the darkness the previous night and went straight to the front door.

He rang the bell, but there was no answer. He rang again and again until at last he heard footsteps. He backed away when the door opened, and Matheson Bell stood with his hand on it.

"Well?" he barked.

"Good evening," Rollison said.

"Who—oh." He peered closer. "Rollison. I'm sorry, Rollison, but I can't spare you any time tonight. There's a family crisis going on, and it's not likely to be settled quickly. I've no time at all to talk."

"You would have to spare time if I were from the police," Rollison said.

"Well, you're not."

Rollison said: "They would very much like me to telephone them and tell them that it would be worthwhile looking under the soil in the monkey-house, wouldn't they?"

Bell actually staggered back, he was so astounded.

"Shall I come in?" asked Rollison. He went forward. "You don't need telling that the police are watching the house and know I'm here, do you?" He stepped inside the hall, past Bell who seemed too flabbergasted to speak or move. He looked as shocked as he would if he knew that the Lopez's were buried in the garden.

Were they?

Chapter Twenty-One

Monkey-House

Very slowly, Bell closed the door. As he did so, his wife appeared from the library and Nora bobbed up just behind her. The evidence of strain on all their faces was so great that yet again Rollison felt sorry for them. He recalled everything he had seen and heard of Nora, including her despondency when she had walked away from the Common. But wouldn't anyone be despondent in such circumstances?

"He knows," Bell said.

"But he can't!" exclaimed Nora.

"How does he know?" asked Charlotte Bell.

All three of them were looking at Rollison. He told himself that with the police outside there was nothing to worry about, and yet it was an odd feeling, to stand here with his back to the closed door and to feel that each one was staring like this: the stillness reminded him of what it was like up in that room of spiders on the first floor – the room from which two venomous insects had been stolen.

"Does it matter how?" asked Bell. "He knows. Why haven't you told the police, Rollison?"

"I thought it might be an advantage to talk about it first."

Bell said roughly: "If you mean you think you can blackmail me, you've another think coming. Someone's already working on that angle. We can't even pay him off, and he doesn't want money in the sense that you know money."

"I was thinking of helping you to pay him the thousand he wants by noon tomorrow," Rollison said.

Nora started, and exclaimed aloud, but her mother stopped her before she could put a question. Bell looked incredulous.

"I want to know whether Cato is working for himself or whether anyone else is behind this," went on Rollison. "It's worth investing a thousand pounds to find out."

"Investing," echoed BelL

His wife moved forward briskly. "I think you owe us some kind of explanation, Mr. Rollison. Why on earth should you help my husband to pay the blackmailer?"

"Shouldn't you make the explanations?" asked Rollison mildly.

"I don't disagree about that," said Charlotte Bell. She turned to her husband. "Mat, I think we ought to telephone the police and get it over. Sooner or later they'll have to know, and the longer we wait the more difficult it will be to convince them that we didn't kill the Lopezes and didn't bury them ourselves." Rollison showed no sign that although he had guessed the truth, he hadn't known it.

"The risk of waiting is too great." Charlotte put her hand to her forehead as she went on: "It was a terrible mistake to pay Cato anything in the first place. A terrible mistake. I'm sure it would be just as wrong to make any arrangement with Mr. Rollison."

Nora said in a whisper: "If only you hadn't." She was looking at her father in a way that was almost hostile.

"The only advantage of telling the police now will be that Cato won't come for his thousand pounds, so we won't be able to find out whether he takes the money to anyone else or whether he means to flee the country with it," Rollison said. "Will it help if I give you a note saying that I asked you to hold off telling the police for twenty-four hours? It's the kind of thing they expect from me."

"Why should you get yourself into serious trouble for us?"

"I think I could talk my way out of it," Rollison replied. "And if you didn't kill the Lopezes, you've nothing to worry about in the long run. Some embarrassment, a little unpleasantness, and then you can go off on one of your expeditions. The jungle folk won't be very worried about what you did or did not do in London. Of course if you did kill them—"

"Of course we didn't," Nora said sharply.

"Nora—"

"Mother, I can't keep quiet any longer. This is another kind of blackmail. How do we know we can believe what he says any more than we can believe Cato? *We've* nothing to be thankful to the Toff for." Her eyes were sparkling angrily. "How does he know about the thousand pounds *if Cato didn't tell him?*"

Her mother caught her breath.

Bell exclaimed: "Good God!"

Rollison laughed. "Very nicely argued," he said. "Do you happen to remember the man and the redhead who went to cover out on the Common just now? Cato had his back to them. The man wore a cloth cap and a choker which didn't seem at all like anything I would wear. The redhead played an unusual kind of gooseberry while I listened in."

"Good heavens!" exclaimed Nora. "I do remember!"

"Cato is being followed now, but the real test will be when he comes for the money tomorrow," Rollison went on.

"I think we ought to go and sit down," said Charlotte Bell. "I don't feel that I can stand any more of this." She led the way into the library and the others followed her. Bell went across to a bureau on which was whisky, a soda syphon and some glasses. He poured out three whiskies and handed one to his wife.

"Help yourself to soda," he said to Rollison.

"I don't understand why you should want to help us like this," Nora said stubbornly.

"I don't know that I want to help you," Rollison replied. "I want to find out whether Cato is working on his own or with someone else. The possible someone else is my real interest. Have you heard the radio tonight?"

"No."

"Then you don't know that Professor Slimm has been charged with Estino's murder," said Rollison.

Bell exclaimed: "Slimm!" He tossed his drink down. "Good God!" That was his habitual expression when he was at a loss for words. "Slimm, Estino and ourselves all involved now. And Cato." He ran his hands nervously over his close-clipped hair.

"If you're trying to help Sammy then you're against my father," said Nora. She seemed determined not to yield an inch. It seemed to Rollison that she was being driven by some anxiety which went even deeper than anything he already knew about. Like Sammy's, her worries had been going on for some time.

"You're still on the ball," Rollison said mildly. "But as I told Sammy, I'm on his side only if he told me the truth. He says he didn't kill Estino. He didn't say anything about the Lopezes, because we – or at least I – didn't know they were dead until just now." Rollison sipped his drink. "Cato says that your father killed Estino and forced him to take the body to Hampstead Heath. Did you know that was going to be his story?"

Charlotte Bell sat down heavily. Her daughter moved to her side, rested a hand on her shoulder and said: "Oh this is terrible. Terrible." She stared at her father, not at Rollison. Bell himself finished off his drink, and said: "You're uncanny, I will say that for you. Well I didn't kill Estino, and I didn't force Cato to, either. I did come back here, though. I had an urgent message from the Lopezes saying that Estino was here and wanted to talk to me. I got back, and found Estino's body up in that room. Cato was here. He said he'd just come and discovered this – he blamed the Lopezes, who weren't here. That was the moment I lost my head. I helped Cato to take the body away. I let him use my car. I even paid him five hundred pounds. I didn't want the police here. For one thing I didn't want my wife and daughter worried. For another I didn't want anything to stop us going off on our next expedition. That's vital to us." He pressed his hands against his forehead. "Or it seemed to be, then. I went back and collected my wife and Nora. We heard nothing from Cato until an hour or so ago, when he said he wanted to talk to Nora. He said on the telephone that he knew that I had killed the Lopezes and they were buried under the monkey-house here. I went out to have a look. There's some newly-dug earth, which has been trampled down.

"After that I simply had to tell the others," went on Bell gruffly. "We just don't know what to do, but Nora agreed to be ready to go to talk to Cato. You heard what he said." Bell began to pace about the room. "My wife is right, of course. I should have told the police in the beginning, and I'll have to tell them now. That puts paid to the most profitable trip we ever expected to make."

He moved across to the telephone, obviously determined in his course of action.

Rollison said: "Let me, will you?" He picked up the receiver and dialled, with all three of them watching that he dialled Whitehall 1212. He asked for Grice, and was told that Grice was at the Wimbledon Police Station. He dialled Wimbledon, still watched silently, and after a pause spoke to Grice.

"Bill, I've got some information about the Bell family which you ought to have," said Rollison, "but I don't want you to have it until tomorrow."

Grice said: "I can't play along, Rolly."

"You can watch the house, in fact you can surround it, if you like," Rollison urged. "The Bells will undertake not to leave it. They know you could hold them at any time for being involved in Estino's murder, and you could pick up all or any one of them if they stepped outside. You can't lose, Bill. Give this a try."

For the first time Nora Bell really seemed to warm towards him; the glow in her eyes reminded him of what she had looked like when she had first met him.

Grice said coldly: "I'll give you until noon tomorrow."

"Two o'clock, Bill. Please."

"All right," said Grice, reluctantly. "I suppose you know what you're doing. But if they step outside their house they'll be arrested and well move in."

"That's understood," Rollison said. "And that's another thing I'll always be grateful to you for." He rang off, turned to the others and went on: "So far, so good. Now I think I'd like to have a look at the monkey-house."

Bell took him out to the back garden. The strong wire cages which he had just seen in the darkness the previous night showed up much more clearly, but it was so nearly dusk that the animals in the cages had settled down for the night. None of them looked at Rollison or Bell as they walked round the gravel paths. Most of the monkeys were very small, but there were one or two fairly big ones.

In one cage two pythons were curled up like a single coil of thick rope.

"This is where the ground has been dug recently," Bell said. He stopped at one of the monkey cages, unlocked it and stepped inside. Rollison followed. The monkey stench was overpowering, but Bell did not seem to notice it. Rollison tried to hold his breath from time to time as Bell cleared a patch of dirt and gravel with his feet, then picked up a spade and began to clear it more. He revealed an outline, about seven feet square, of a patch of newly-dug earth. It had been trampled down and then smoothed over, so that the footprints hardly showed. The soil within the patch was much easier to push a spade into than the soil round the perimeter.

"It's a hideous thought that they're buried here," Bell said. "I keep telling myself that it can't be true."

"We can soon find out," said Rollison.

"How?"

"Dig down until we find something," Rollison said.

Bell stood in front of rum, tight lipped. Rollison studied the good-looking face, trying to make up his mind whether the idea was really repugnant to him, or whether he hated the thought of digging down to corpses which he himself had buried. Suddenly, Bell turned away.

"I'll get a fork," he said.

It took them fifteen minutes to dig down to something which had a different substance from that of the soil. By chance, they came upon the faces. When he saw them, swollen and discoloured, Bell said in a tense voice: "You know what happened to them, don't you?"

"No. What?"

"They were bitten by a tarantula. That's unmistakable. Some devil turned a spider loose on them."

Rollison didn't speak, but stared back at the house where the lights were going on at the back. He was not thinking of the women in the house, however; he was thinking of the way Cato had broken down under the threat of having snakes or spiders brought to Cellar 3. If Cato's dread of the venomous reptiles and insects was genuine, then it was almost impossible that he had killed the two people buried here.

"We'd better fill that in and get back," said Rollison, gruffly.

Bell didn't speak, but began to shovel back the soil.

There was a curious unreality about the next hour. Charlotte and Nora Bell made some sandwiches and coffee, and Rollison realised how hungry he was. They looked at the late-night news on B.B.C. television, and there was a picture of Sammy Slimm. It showed only for a second or two, and the announcer went off into a story about football in Brazil. As the minutes ticked by to midnight, the women became more restless. The clock in the hall struck twelve, and for two minutes afterwards the tension was almost unbearable.

The telephone bell rang.

Matheson Bell went to it, slowly, and took off the receiver.

"Yes?" he said.

He listened. He said: "Yes, I'll find it somehow … Where? … How? … Yes, if she can." There was a longer pause, before he went on savagely: "If I can't get it I can't get it. I will if I can!"

He banged the receiver down, and turned to Rollison.

"He will be at Piccadilly Circus underground station tomorrow at twelve noon. He wants the money in one-pound notes in a small suitcase. He wants Nora to take it to him, but if the police won't let Nora leave—"

"We'll fix that," Rollison said confidently. "Now I'm going home."

That night he slept what Wrightson would have called the sleep of the just. Nothing disturbed him except an odd dream, of a girl with a beautiful head of auburn hair with Marta's face beneath it.

He woke just after eight o'clock, breakfasted by nine and talked to the hospital, to Sammy Slimm's lawyer and to Bill Ebbutt before going to see Grice by appointment. This time he was escorted up to Grice's office, as if authority had said that he must not be allowed the freedom of the Yard.

"Bill," said Rollison when the door was closed, "one day I hope to find a way of saying thanks for the tip you gave me yesterday. Here's a little in earnest. The Bells are being blackmailed. Their daughter is to take a thousand pounds in one-pound notes to the blackmailer at Piccadilly Circus station today at noon. Will you let her leave the house with the money?"

"Where is she going to get the money from?

"I'm going to get it for her."

Grice said: "You really are determined to go all the way in this job, aren't you?" He considered. "All right, but I'll have to pick her up for questioning immediately afterwards. If this is an attempt to get her away from the house, you will have had your last concession from me."

"And rightly," said Rollison. "I'm going straight to my bank from here. Then I'm going out to Wimbledon again, and I'll be at Piccadilly by the time the girl arrives."

"All right," said Grice. "Have you been to the Marigold Club this morning?"

"No."

"Marta Estino is almost normal again," Grice told him. "She is very subdued but also very positive. She's read through and signed a statement which we drew up after yesterday's interview. Lady Gloria seems to think she is very much in love with Sliinm. And our people at Cannon Row, where we're holding Slimm, seem to think he's obsessed by her."

"I think they're dead right," said Rollison.

"Do you also think Slimm did kill Estino?"

"It's one of the things we have to find out," Rollison said prosaically.

He was at his bank just after a quarter past ten. The manager was not at all surprised that he should draw out so much ready cash. He took this in a tailor's suit-box to Wimbledon.

None of the Bells seemed to have slept well, but Rollison spent ten minutes with Matheson Bell on his own. Then he left for the first part of the journey with Nora. She said very little, just sat staring ahead; he was vividly reminded of her despondency on the Common.

"I'm going to drop you at Putney Bridge Station," he said at last. "You can get a train to the Piccadilly Line from there, and you'll be in good time. You simply go up to Cato and hand him the box. Don't do anything else. Your father's checked it, and it contains the money exactly as Cato demanded it."

"I wish I knew why you're doing all this," Nora said.

Rollison said, gently: "It's a matter of faith, Nora."

She started. *"Faith?"*

Rollison was looking at some traffic slowing down before a set of traffic lights.

"Yes," he said. "Faith is an old friend of mine. I don't really believe that Sammy Slimm is involved, but he could be. Do you really think your father is involved? Is that what's frightening you so much?"

She didn't answer, but when he glanced at her he judged from the heightened colour that she did fear that her father knew more than he had admitted.

Chapter Twenty-Two

£1,000 Plus

The next time Rollison saw Nora she was walking slowly round the arcade at Piccadilly Circus station, carrying the box by the cardboard handle, as if she had just come away from a shop. Rollison, his back to her, could see her in a small mirror in a window advertising cosmetics. She looked very sturdy and very wholesome – he kept thinking about that word where the Bells were concerned. Then he remembered her walking away from the Common, head down, distress in her whole being. She must be just as distressed now, but her shoulders were squared and she held her head high.

What was passing through her mind? Suspicion of her father? Or even certainty that he knew more than he had admitted?

Rollison turned so that he could see more clearly, and then saw a young bearded man approach her. Something about the way the man walked warned him that this was Cato, but the girl had no idea. The beard was thick and dark, and Cato also wore a wig. He passed the girl, then turned and followed her. Rollison also followed, more slowly. Cato waited until the girl was near one of the exits leading up to Piccadilly Circus, and spoke to her.

Two men who were looking at magazines at the bookstall turned round now, and a third, who had been walking aimlessly after Nora, drew closer to her. She started, and then turned. Face to face with the bearded man she obviously realised who it was. She drew back a pace and raised her free hand, as if to fend something off. Alarm flared through Rollison's mind that Cato was going to attack her.

Cato simply held out his hand. Slowly, reluctantly, Nora gave him the cardboard box. His words just carried to Rollison: "Wait a minute."

He held the box on one arm and began to prise up the lid, obviously to make sure that it contained what he wanted. He got it open a fraction of an inch, and no one appeared to take any notice of the pair standing there. A crowd of trippers came noisily out of the escalators, an American voice loud and clear, a Lancastrian voice responding. Oblivious of all this, Cato opened the box wider.

Then he cried out, dropped it, and staggered away. As he did so, a spider dropped out of the box, huge, dark, furry. Some of the women in the party saw it and screamed. Cato, face ashen grey above the black beard, banged into one of the big men, who gripped his shoulder. The spider scuttled along towards the crowd. Suddenly there was a panic and a wild rush towards the staircase. Women were screaming and men shouting until Rollison's voice rose high above them all.

"It's harmless! Don't panic. It's harmless!"

Then a man with huge feet trod on the creature. A woman fainted, a man sounded as if he were sick.

Cato was now between two Yard men, and the third was holding the box with the money in it.

Rollison joined Nora.

Cato, still looking sick and pale, had recovered enough to glare at the girl and say viciously: "Now your father will hang. That's what you've done for him."

"That's enough," said the Yard man on his right "See you later, Mr. Rollison."

Rollison nodded. Rollison took Nora's arm, but she freed herself and looked at him with unveiled hostility. Her father came hurrying from the telephone booths, and Charlotte Bell from a tobacco kiosk. The crowd had quietened, for police were reasoning, reassuring them. The police also made it easy for Rollison and the Bells to go up the Swan and Edgar subway. Rollison hailed a taxi and within five minutes they were entering his flat. Wrightson was dressed in a suit borrowed from Jolly.

"Keep out of earshot, Percy," ordered Rollison.

"You knew that the police were going to be there," Nora accused when they were in the big room. "You didn't want Cato to get away."

"I thought you wanted to follow him," Charlotte Bell put in.

"I knew that the police wouldn't take the risk of letting me," admitted Rollison. "And I needed to find out something else, something vital. Your father knows what it was. You should, too."

"Well I don't."

"Did you have to put the spider in the box to make sure Cato couldn't get away?" asked Charlotte.

Bell said: "No, he didn't. He simply wanted to find out whether Cato really hated poisonous spiders, and was frightened of them. He is frightened all right. So it isn't likely that he put the snakes and the spider in Rollison's flat, and not likely that he handled them when they killed the Lopezes. Cato used the gun, that's all. If we only had the shooting to worry about we might have the right man, but you know there's someone else, Rollison, don't you?"

Rollison looked at him levelly.

"I'm quite sure there is."

Charlotte said in a low-pitched voice: "Oh, Mat."

Nora was biting her lips.

"You know, you two," said Bell in a low-pitched voice, "it's bad enough to be suspected by Rollison and the police, and worse to have a charge of murder hanging over me. But the worst thing of all is that my wife and daughter believe that I might have had anything to do with this beastliness." He was looking at his wife, who did not shift her gaze. "That's almost more than I can take."

"If only you hadn't come back from Paris," Nora said.

"Well, I did come back. And you know why."

"Which is more than I do," said Rollison. "It might help if I did."

Bell said: "Can I have that drink now?" He watched Rollison pour out, without saying another word. The women refused a drink.

Rollison had a weak whisky, not because he wanted it, but because it was no time for Bell to drink alone.

Bell finished his drink and took out his wallet, extracted a flimsy piece of paper and spread it out. He moved it so he could place it on the big desk. Rollison went nearer, but Charlotte and her daughter obviously knew what it was, and were not greatly interested.

It was a map, very lightly drawn; when Rollison drew nearer he saw that it was a carbon copy. The lines were pale grey and the paper was faintly blue.

"This is it," Bell said. "It's a map of the Old Palace Gardens of Arodia. The place is in ruins, and has been for nearly a century. Buried deep beneath one of the temples of the palace are the old crown jewels of Arodia. The priests who hid them left colonies of poisonous spiders to protect them, and because of the spiders no one has gone near those remains for nearly a hundred years. In some places there are snake pits as well. A few of the sacred monkeys, the Simis, are also there. We all went for the specimens and found the treasure. We were all ready to dig it up and share it – Estino, Sammy Slimm and me. Cato was to get a smaller cut, because he flew us about so often and he knew what we were after. But we were driven away by the fighting. That damned war! Cato stayed to report exactly what was happening out there, but he didn't know where the jewels were hidden. Estino had a map like this, so did Sammy, so did I. As far as I know there were only the three in existence. Those jewels are worth millions of pounds, Rollison. There is a roof of an old temple buried in one of the cellars – a roof made of beaten gold which had been put on in layers year after year through the centuries. We know it's there. I've actually been down in the hiding-place. I've seen it all. I brought a few jewels back, as samples. When we were forced to leave we all pledged ourselves to go back together in a joint expedition. But someone decided that he wanted everything for himself. That's all I can tell you. Everything. For the rest – I've told you the truth. I did come back from Paris, and I did find Estino dead and Cato here. The knowledge that millions of pounds worth of jewels were waiting for me in Arodia if I kept silent was the deciding factor. It's all very well for you and Nora to say that it wasn't worth it." Bell went on. "At the time it seemed well worth five hundred pounds to have Cato on my side, as well as to get rid of Estino's body. If I had to do the same thing over again, I wouldn't change anything. I would take the chance." He looked at his wife and daughter steadily.

Rollison said, quite gently: "But someone killed Estino and someone killed the Lopezes. Cato may have killed Estino, but it's pretty clear that he didn't kill the servants or work on my flat."

"I know what you're thinking," Bell said. "It must have been Sammy Slimm or me. You've a lot of faith in Sammy, so you would prefer to think that it was me."

Rollison murmured: "Unless you were in it together, of course."

No one else spoke. Bell did not look away from Rollison, but his eyes were narrowed, as if he were frightened.

Nora began to move about the room. She came to a standstill by the trophy wall, staring at it as if she was glad to have somewhere else to look except at her father.

The telephone bell rang, a sharp relief from the tension. Rollison moved to pick it up. Everyone was watching him, and he knew that they wondered if this was the police. He hoped that it was Lady Gloria, whom he had telephoned from Putney after leaving Nora at the station.

"Well, Richard," said Lady Gloria. "For better or worse, we have done what you asked. Maggie will be at your flat in a few minutes, with Marta Estino. I charge you not to distress that child any more than is absolutely necessary."

"That's a promise," Rollison said. "Thank you, Glory."

"Let me know just as quickly as you can what it is all about," Lady Gloria said.

Rollison said: "Yes, I will." He rang off, turned to look at the others, and went on: "A mutual friend is coming to see us and I don't mean the police." He went to the door leading to the domestic quarters, opened it and called: "Percy!"

"Yes, sir."

"When there is a ring at the front door, I'll answer it. You stay where you are."

"Very good, sir," said Wrightson, almost certainly disappointed.

A minute after he had answered there was a ring at the front door bell. Rollison went out, watched with painful interest by the Bell family. He deliberately increased the tension. He wanted it to be at screaming pitch when these three people met Marta Estino.

He glanced up at a kind of periscope mirror which Jolly had installed and which was an ever-present aid in time of danger. He saw Maggie and Marta, by themselves. He opened the door and stood aside. Marta looked at him gravely. She was in that same white and off-white skirt and jumper, and the most remarkable thing about her was the purity of her complexion.

"How are you, Rolly?" Maggie asked.

"Fine," said Rollison. "I'm glad you could both come. Wait here a minute, Maggie, will you?" He took Marta's arm and led her towards the big room. He thrust the door open and let her go in first.

There was a startled silence. Then:"*Marta!*" exclaimed Charlotte Bell.

"Marta," said Rollison, moving quickly after the girl, "Sammy Slimm is already under arrest for the murder of your father. Now Mr. Bell is faced with the charge of murdering the Lopezes, the servants at his house. You know what did happen, don't you? You know who did kill the servants. It was your father, wasn't it? Your father killed them and buried them. Which of his friends helped to bury them? Was it Sammy Slimm? Was it Matheson Bell? Or was it someone else? And—which of them killed *him?*"

Chapter Twenty-Three

Killer

Maggie was hovering in the doorway, as if she thought that Marta would collapse. Nora and Charlotte Bell did not move, but watched the girl as if their very lives depended on her answer; as in a way they did. Rollison kept a hand on the girl's arm, a little afraid that she might try to free herself and run away. Once before under terrible pressure her mind had suffered a strange transition, shock had driven her to walk blindly about this part of London. Was this a big enough shock to have the same effect again?

"Did your father kill the Lopezes?" insisted Rollison, in a very clear voice.

Marta said slowly, painfully: "Yes. Yes, he did. But he did not mean to kill them. He meant only to frighten them. They knew about the jewels in the old palace, you see." She paused, but there seemed no danger of collapse, she seemed quite rational. "They told us that they heard you telling your wife and daughter, Mr. BelL When we arrived, after you had gone, they demanded the map from us. My father tried to frighten them. He believed that the spiders he used for that had been rendered harmless, their poison sac removed. But the cages had been changed. They were poisonous spiders, after all. The man and woman died. While they were there, Max Cato arrived. Already Mr. Bell was on his way back to see us, because he had telephoned and my father had told him what the servants were doing."

She stopped again and closed her eyes, but did not falter when she went on: "Already, Sammy had been to see me. He was not very interested in the jewels, he was very interested in me. Just in me. And I loved him much, also. I wished—I wished my father would change his mind about our marriage. I wanted to marry Sammy so very, very much. When he had gone, and we were alone, before Cato came and before Mr. Bell arrived, I went to protest to my father. But I did not know then that while I had been out he had killed the Lopezes. That was why he had been in such a terrible temper. He was beside himself. I could see that there was dirt on his clothes and that he had been busy, but I did not know at first that the Lopezes were dead.

"I held Sammy's gun.

"I told my father that if he would not allow me to marry Sammy Slimm, then I would kill myself."

She stopped. She closed her eyes. She lowered her face into her cupped hands and stood like that in an attitude of prayer and of weeping. When she spoke again the words were hardly audible, and yet each one was clear because each one was so vital to their needs.

"Never have I seen him in such a rage. Soon I was able to understand why, but at the time it was just terrible. At last he told me he had killed the Lopezes. He told me he had buried them. He told me that he would kill Sammy, also. He told me he did not care if I killed myself. He frightened me. In the name of God I tell you that he frightened me. He came towards me, his eyes like fire. In my hand was the gun, and my hand moved. So—I saw my father die."

She stood so still that she looked like a figure turned to stone, but soon another sentence seemed to whisper about her hands.

"After that I do not remember. I do not remember. But this I know. When I saw Sammy at a strange place, he told me to say nothing to you, he said he would look after everything. So—so until now I have not told anyone. Not anyone at all."

Sammy Slimm and Matheson Bell and Max Cato remembered, however, and when their stories were all told they made a comprehensive one which Grice related to Rollison, later that day.

The weather had changed and the Thames outside Grice's window looked leaden and was whipping up like a young sea. No pleasure craft ventured out. The Yard was quiet, too, for the evening hush was settling upon it: the time was half past six.

"She didn't get the story in quite the right order," Grice said. "And she didn't know that Cato – who had come to get an advance on his share of the value of the jewels, under threat of telling the world about them – was present when her father killed the Lopezes. Estino had tried to frighten Cato, too. When Estino was dead and Marta had collapsed, Cato went in and sized up the situation. It looked perfect to him. Everyone was in his hands, he could blackmail them one after the other or simultaneously, as he chose. He started on Bell, whose first consideration was to get rid of the body. Bell didn't know that the Lopezes had been killed – it wasn't until Cato demanded the thousand pounds last night that the family realised that."

"And it shook them," Rollison murmured.

"It's a pity it didn't shake you," said Grice drily. "They didn't know that he wanted enough money to get out of the country and to be low for a while. You had scared him badly at Ebbutt's place."

"Bill," said Rollison earnestly, "I'm sure that Ebbutt could find fifty witnesses to say that Cato stayed there of his own free will. I would hate you to think that it was a matter of coercion."

Grice shook his head, very slowly. "You're incorrigible," he said. "Perhaps that's just as well. Now that we know Cato's story of course the rest fits in. He talked freely on the way from Piccadilly yesterday, that spider really shook him, and he didn't get his confidence back until he had talked much more than he ever expected to. He wanted to kill Marta Estino, of course, because – well, how about a guess?" Grice broke off, and sat smugly at his desk as if confident that Rollison would not even try.

"Guess?" echoed Rollison. "Or simple deduction? She was the one person who knew the true story of the murder of the Lopezes and Estino, and who could let the Bells and later Sammy Slimm off the hook for those murders. She could free them and damn him. So the quicker he could get rid of her, the better. And when the attack failed, he turned on me. He thought that if he could scare me—"

Rollison stopped, because Grice, who had started to look impressed, now began to grin derisively. Rollison put his head on one side, and demanded: "What's funny?"

"You are, Rolly. It's nice to know you can boob sometimes. Cato did try to kill Marta Estino by shooting her with the gun he had taken from Wimbledon – Sammy Slimm's gun, incidentally, and Cato knew that. He also tossed that scorpion into your car – he screwed himself up to do that – the thing was in a paper container which broke when it hit the car seat. He had brought it from *Faraway*, where there are a number of scorpions. But Cato did not attack Jolly or leave the snakes or the spiders at your flat. Incidentally, I have two papers here. Perhaps you'd like to look at them."

Grice pushed them across. The top one was a laboratory report headed:

Report on remains of reptiles and spider found at the home of the Honourable Richard Rollison: 2 common English adders, poison extracted before death. 1 Tarantula spider, poison sac removed before death.

The report was signed by a Home Office analyst and countersigned by Horace Wall.

"Well, well," said Rollison. "So whoever put those in my flat didn't mean to kill me."

"And the man who attacked Jolly didn't intend to kill him," said Grice.

"Not Sammy Slimm," said Rollison in a protesting voice.

"Sammy Slimm," affirmed Grice, positively. "He knew that Marta had killed her father – in fact he is prepared to swear that it was in self-defence, and I don't think there's much doubt about that. He got her away from Wimbledon and sent her to a hotel to wait for him, while he went back to try to clear up the mess. Instead, he got further involved, and Marta went wandering, shocked out of her mind. Then Slimm realised that the whole truth would come out sooner or later. He thought you would find a way to cover it all up if *you* found it out fast. So he involved you by putting the snakes and the spider in your flat."

Rollison said heavily: "I could forgive him for that. I could even forgive him for not coming and telling me the whole story. It's much harder to forgive him for attacking Jolly, *and* running him down."

"I don't know whether you'll ever be convinced," said Grice, "but he swears that he only meant to knock Jolly out. He hurt him more than he realised, and took him to the spot where he was found and telephoned the police to tell them about it. He wanted Jolly in hospital as quickly as he could get him there, and he wasn't sure when you would be back. He says the car door slammed on Jolly's leg when he was getting him out, and he'd left the brake off and a wheel almost went over Jolly's legs."

Rollison said heavily: "I hope Jolly believes him." He was acutely aware of his own misgivings about Sammy Slimm. After this he would never wholly trust the man, but perhaps there was no particular reason why he should ever have to.

"Slimm says that he called you soon after you'd got back, but lacked the nerve to talk to you then, and rang off without a word," Grice went on. "Did you have a call?"

"Yes," said Rollison, still heavily. He put the laboratory report on one side, and looked at the second. It was a typewritten statement, signed by Sammy Slimm, admitting everything that Grice had just reported. He emphasised that just before drugging Marta he had told her to say nothing, to leave everything to him.

"What will happen to Sammy?" Rollison asked.

"We can charge him with the attack on Jolly," Grice answered. "You needn't make the charge yourself. He'll probably get six months for that. Don't you think he should?"

"I certainly do think he should," said Rollison, heavily. "What about Marta?"

"I don't think we're likely to make a charge against her," replied Grice. "All the evidence, including the statement from Cato, suggested that she was genuinely terrified of her father, who had gone almost berserk that night. We'll probably have a lot of difficulty proving intent to kill, and even then self-defence would probably clear her. We've got Cato for attempted murder, of course; he'll get the maximum sentence." In fact, Rollison realised that Cato would spend at least ten years in prison.

"The Bells come out of this cleaner than most, but not altogether clean," Grice went on. "I don't think we'll press any charges even if we could frame any that would stick. But Bell himself was quite prepared to cover up murder in order to get his share of the Arodia jewels. Those jewels *have* officially been lost for a hundred years," Grice went on. "I've had a word with the Arodian Embassy, and they're tickled to death about the discovery. It's the biggest single contribution to their exchequer this year. That's what I mean by saying that even the Bells didn't come out of it clean – all three of them were prepared to help to bring the jewels out of the country which owned them."

"Hmm," said Rollison.

"Don't you agree?"

"Oh, absolutely," Rollison said. "I was just wondering how many people would possess a social conscience disciplined well enough to take a different attitude. The Bells could argue that if the money had lain buried for a hundred years it might have stayed there for another hundred if these particular people hadn't found it. I'm not offering that as an excuse, mind you. Just as a fact."

"Your social conscience would be disciplined well enough," said Grice drily.

Rollison smiled at him with genuine affection.

"Thank you for that and everything else, Bill," he said warmly. "But remember I have enough money to get along with, and the Bells have hardly enough to keep their expeditions going. However – if the Arodian Government gave a reward to the finders it might help. I used to go to school with the second prince in line of succession. I'll have a word with him. He'll know Sammy, too."

"I shouldn't remind him of that," said Grice.

Three months later Cato was sentenced to ten years imprisonment and Sammy Slimm to three months, a short term largely because

Jolly made a special plea for him and Rollison made great play of the fact that Sammy had tried to make sure that Jolly got medical attention as quickly as possible. His counsel made great play, also, with a statement that when Sammy had gone to Hampstead Heath he had been following Cato – to find out what he was doing.

Marta did not attend the trial. The Bell family did, Matheson Bell to give evidence, Charlotte and Nora as spectators. Afterwards they went round to Rollison's flat for a drink. Nora looked younger, brighter and much happier.

"How's Marta?" inquired Rollison, for Marta was staying with them.

"I don't think she'll ever forget what happened, but I think she's stopped blaming herself," said Charlotte. "She's desperately in love with Sammy, you know. If she'd had her way she would have married him while he was awaiting trial, but he wouldn't agree. A remarkable thing has happened, by the way," Charlotte went on. "Tell him. Mat."

Nora, studying the trophy wall, had come to a standstill.

"The Arodian Government has asked us to make a joint expedition out there," said Bell. "They will pay all expenses for twelve months for the lot of us. My agent Bryer thinks it's the surest seller ever. He's back from Hollywood, by the way – he really does exist. Someone sold the idea that we were going to turn over the jewels to them once we had found them."

"I wonder who that was," murmured Rollison.

"You know very well who it was," said Lady Gloria, coming from the kitchen quarters. Rollison had not known that she was here. Jolly, back on duty and in full health, had obviously been instructed not to tell him. "It was you yourself. I see no reason why you should hide that kind of light under a bushel. I'm delighted to hear that Marta is well, Mrs. Bell. I hope you'll bring her to tea at the Marigold Club soon. Then—"

Lady Gloria broke off, as if shocked. She put up her lorgnette and studied Nora Bell as Nora put her arms round Rollison and hugged him.

"Dear me," said Lady Gloria.

A week later, Marta, Nora and Charlotte went to tea with Lady Gloria and Maggie. They were waited on by a girl with a wonderful head of red hair, and a complexion almost as good as Marta's.

"I seem to remember seeing her before somewhere," said Nora. "I can't place her, though." After a pause, she went on: "Lady Gloria, do you think the Toff would like a spider or a snake for his trophy wall? A stuffed one, of course. I'd rather like to think he had one there."

"I will ask him," said Lady Gloria.

"Richard," she said on the telephone that evening, "Nora Bell would like to bring you a stuffed tarantula for your trophy wall. I hope you won't accept. I should shudder every time I entered your flat. You needn't answer at once, anyhow. There is one other thing. The young woman you insist on calling Ginger appears to be shaping up very well. Has Nora Bell met her before?"

"Vaguely, I believe," Rollison said. "She was able to help me on the case, and I sent her to France for a holiday. When she came back she asked for a job in which she could learn to improve herself. Where else should I send her but the Marigold Club?"

"I have a feeling that she is a young baggage," said Lady Gloria. "However, I will improve her out of all knowledge. Have no fear of that."

JOHN CREASEY

GIDEON'S DAY

Gideon's day is a busy one. He balances family commitments with solving a series of seemingly unrelated crimes from which a plot nonetheless evolves and a mystery is solved.

One of the most senior officers within Scotland Yard, George Gideon's crime solving abilities are in the finest traditions of London's world famous police headquarters. His analytical brain and sense of fairness is respected by colleagues and villains alike.

'The finest of all Scotland Yard series' – New York Times.

GIDEON'S FIRE

Commander George Gideon of Scotland Yard has to deal successively with news of a mass murderer, a depraved maniac, and the deaths of a family in an arson attack on an old building south of the river. This leaves little time for the crisis developing at home ....

'Gideon of Scotland Yard emerges as one of the most real working detectives in modern fiction.... A sympathetic and believable professional policeman.' - New York Times

JOHN CREASEY

THE CREEPERS

"The prisoner's hand was thin and bony ... And in the centre of the palm was a pinkish mark. It was the shape of a wolf's head, mouth open, fangs showing. Although it was what he had expected to see, Inspector West felt a twinge of repugnance a stab not unrelated to fear. It was the fifth time he had seen the mark of the wolf – the mark of Lobo."

A gang of cat burglars led by Lobo cause mayhem as they terrorize the city. They must be stopped, but with little in the way of evidence the police are baffled. Just how can Inspector West manage to do this in what is a race against time before more victims succumb?

"Here is an excellent novel of law enforcement officers, harried, discouraged and desperately fatigued, moving inexorably ahead under the pressure of knowledge that they must succeed to save human lives." - Cleveland Plain-Dealer

"Furiously exciting" - Chicago Tribune

"The action is fast, continuous and exciting" - San Francisco News

John Creasey

Introducing the Toff

Whilst returning home from a cricket match at his father's country home, the Honourable Richard Rollison - alias The Toff - comes across an accident which proves to be a mystery. As he delves deeper into the matter with his usual perseverance and thoroughness , murder and suspense form the backdrop to a fast moving and exciting adventure.

'The Toff has been promoted to a place of honour among amateur detectives.' – The Times Literary Supplement

Case Against Paul Raeburn

Chief Inspector Roger West has been watching and waiting for over two years – he is determined to catch Paul Raeburn out. The millionaire racketeer may have made a mistake, following the killing of a small time crook.

Can the ace detective triumph over the evil Raeburn in what are very difficult circumstances? This cannot be assumed as not evething, it would seem, is as simple as it first appears .....

'Creasey can drive a narrative along like nobody's business ... ingenious plot ... interesting background .' - The Sunday Times

Printed in Great Britain
by Amazon